ROSE'S WRATH

Rose's War Duology #1

Oceane McAllister

Printed in the United States of America

First Printing, 2020

ISBN 9781795503105

www.oceanemcallister.com

To my biggest supporter, Isabel, who has stuck with me from the beginning of the first draft. I anticipate many more moments of fangirling over Bear. *wink*

And to my cousin and friend, Mariana. Thanks for helping with the final edits and for being an A+ Beta reader.

Love you both!

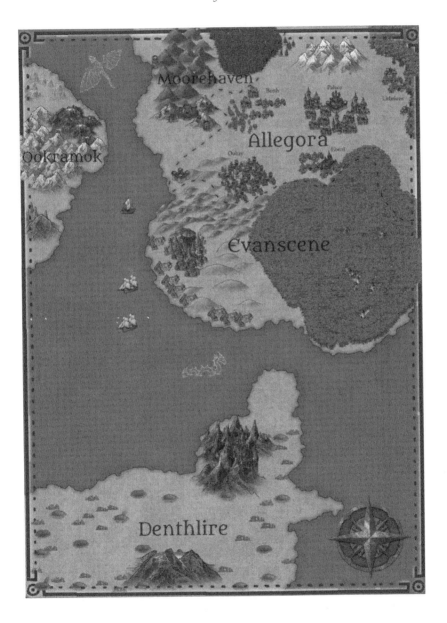

Contents

1

CERISE

THE SCENT OF blood filled Cerise's nostrils, flooding her with panic. Her bare feet slapped over the damp leaves of the forest, muted in comparison to the hammering of her heart.

She thought she could control it, but the fact that she was running for her life spoke of the exact opposite. She most definitely could not control it. Even so, she had to admit she was relieved that Raina was dead.

Dead. A sense of triumph coursed through her body, and a slight grin appeared on her features. She had succeeded.

The sharp crack of a branch caused Cerise to speed up and lose her train of thought; they were almost to her.

The long cloak she had grabbed on her way out of the cottage whipped about her ankles, threatening to trip her. She would have removed it, but unfortunately, she was naked, and they could easily trace her scent with the cloak should she drop it. Another unfortunate part of the rather twisted day.

She wiped her mouth, no longer surprised at the redness that now stained her hand. It was tough not focusing on the iron taste that filled her mouth because it would be far too easy to give in and either throw up or kill someone else. Neither was a welcome thought.

If she could only reach the cave, she'd be fine. Whoever or whatever was following her would be lost in the labyrinth that was a second home to Cerise. Now it was her only home, but she had always preferred it to Raina's mildewy, hark-infested, miserable excuse for a cottage anyway.

Her toe caught on a root, and with a small whimper of pain, she tumbled down. Rolling up out of the fall with agility uncommon among the other eighteen-year-olds of her village, Cerise kept running. She had lost at least three seconds of her lead, though, and she could only hope that there was still enough time.

No one had known about her, except Raina of course, and if others now knew... Cerise shuddered at the thought. Hybrids were illegal in Allegora. To be a hybrid was considered one of the worst crimes, punishable by imprisonment in Denthlire for all eternity. Despite its flaws, Cerise happened to enjoy her life in the forest of Lithrium and had no interest in spending the rest of her life in the land of fog and smoke.

The cave was close, only a few hundred yards away. If she could just make it a little farther…

The loud crack and crumble of a tree's branches in front of her caused Cerise to stumble to a halt. Her stomach dropped at the sight of the shape which now towered over her. They had hired a trigor?

Most people thought their crooked fangs, dripping with poison, to be their most frightening feature, but Cerise found the milky, oozing blobs in place of their eyes more terrifying.

The creature hissed, its large nostrils flaring, trying to pinpoint the scent as it flapped its leathery wings. Cerise looked down at her blood-stained hand and gulped.

They were tracking her with Raina's blood.

Her natural instinct was to shift, but she lost control when she did that. The wolf was easy to become. The human… not so much.

The trigor growled, a weird, high-pitched whine following. Frustration. The scent of her sweat and natural smell must have been masking the smell of blood.

She circled slowly, rubbing as much blood off her hands and mouth with the cloak as possible. She'd have to use it as a distraction. Still, neither fleeing nor fighting were options. It seemed she would have to shift. She closed her eyes, allowing her body to transform. Her muscles remained tense; she hated this, how her bones changed shape, snapping into new places. Cerise bit back a whimper of pain. She didn't shift often enough to grow accustomed to the process. Her paws settled on the leaf-strewn ground, her vision, hearing, and sense of smell increasing. The cloak fluttered down beside the large brown wolf.

Loping away from the cloak, Cerise noted that the trigor had begun clawing its way toward it. She felt her human mentality slipping, but she held onto one thought: Kill the trigor. Hopefully, the wolf would listen.

The wolf skulked behind the trigor, trying to spot its weaknesses. The larger creature tore apart the cloak, its harsh snarls echoing through the forest.

Usually ripping out the throat was the best option, but this creature had a tough, scaly body which would be incredibly difficult to penetrate.

The wolf's eyes roamed over the trigor's body. The body was too strong, the limbs bearing claws were too sharp. But the wings... she could shred its wings.

Stalking from the left, the wolf leaped onto the trigor's back, her teeth snapping and ripping at the leathery material.

The trigor screeched in pain, trying in vain to throw the wolf off. She continued to destroy the trigor's left wing, her claws buried firmly in the back of the scaly creature.

Leaping off, the wolf snapped at the trigor's right wing but was batted back by its whirling tail. The wolf went tumbling into the brush but rose quickly. The trigor was weakened, its balance off. Taking advantage of this, the wolf attacked from below, tearing at the underside of the right wing. A harsh snap and a hoarse cry accompanied the wing breaking. Victory in sight, the wolf prowled around the helpless trigor, which was desperately trying to sense its attacker.

Sludge-like grey blood trickling from its damaged wings, it let out a mournful cry, as if it knew death was near. It was now defenseless, its only hope that it could somehow capture the wolf between its poisonous jaws.

The wolf was unaffected by the creature's plea for mercy. Leaping onto its back once more, the wolf took the trigor's neck in her jaws, relishing the crack of the spine as the creature went limp.

While inspecting her kill, the blackness that clouded the edge of her vision faded, and a low whimper escaped her throat.

Shocked, Cerise could not believe what the wolf had done, what she had done. Why did she remember? Twice now it had happened. She remembered everything from the kill. From both kills, actually. Was it awful that she cared more about this one?

Seeing blood once more made her tremble. She should be used to it by now, though.

12

She moved slightly and realized she was still in wolf form. Her wildly pounding heart coursed fear through her veins. What if she couldn't shift back? The thought of being stuck with a killing mind, bloodied fangs, and a four-legged body... That was a nightmare she could not bear.

Closing her eyes, she willed her body to change. She pictured human legs, a torso, and her curly brown hair.

But nothing. She whined low in her throat, terrified.

Unfortunately, her mother wasn't here to explain. She could have helped Cerise understand why it was increasingly easy to allow the wolf to take control or why she was still herself in her wolf form. But her mother was gone, leading her pack of werewolves, thinking that her daughter was still safe with her father.

The dark form of the trigor caught her eye again, and she flinched. If someone had hired one to track her, then she needed to get to her cave. She trotted away, slowly gaining speed. Cerise had no idea how long her wolf form would last, so the faster she got to the cave, the better.

The narrow crevice in the rock wall was a welcome sight despite the fact that it looked like an entrance to a ligert cavern. The flesh-eating worms were a terrible sight, their sharp mandibles and slimy claws perfect for grabbing prey. Thankfully, there were none in this cave. Most had been captured by the king to use in his army.

Her canine body slid through smoothly, the cave opening up once she was inside. This place was her escape and was more of a home than Raina's cottage had ever been.

She trotted down numerous passages, traveling in a seemingly careless pattern. After about a minute, she approached her room—a large cavern with a small stream winding its way through.

Taking a deep breath, Cerise tried again to shift. Nothing happened. Her limbs began to shake, a low whine escaping her. She just wanted to be herself again. Settling down to the cool floor, she curled up, wanting to fall asleep and pretend that everything was fine.

Cerise opened her eyes quickly, scanning her surroundings. Why was she so cold? Her hands brushed her legs. Human legs, hands... she was human.

Crouched on the ground, her human skin shivering in the cold dampness of the cave, Cerise slowly rose, inspecting the cuts and bruises she had obtained while fighting the trigor. Well, that the wolf had obtained. She didn't want to associate that thing that was inside of her with herself.

Stumbling slowly over to a trunk where she kept spare clothing specifically for times like these, Cerise grabbed warm woolen pants and a linen blouse. She'd never been a fan of gowns, finding them too cumbersome, especially once she shifted. The last time she had worn one while shifting, it had taken her a good ten minutes to escape the three layers.

She also took a cloak that was hanging on an outcropping of the rock wall. It was deep scarlet etched in gold. It bore the mage's crest, a proud dragon spewing a flame of gold. She could still remember her father donning it and how it would billow out as it settled on his shoulders.

Cerise carefully wrapped it around herself, marveling at the richness of it. Her fingers gently caressed the fraying edges, remembering how he would often let her wear it as a child, the hem long enough to be a train. Whenever she wore it now, she thought of him and his radiant smile.

Cerise walked silently over to her bed, which was just a bunch of furs jumbled together. Settling down, the sheer magnitude of what had happened in just the past few hours bore down on Cerise, making her inhale loudly. She had finally killed her—killed the witch who had murdered her father.

2

VERRE

IT WAS TIME. Verre smoothed the shimmering silver folds of her gown, the movement allowing her a peek at her sparkling glass slippers. Glass. The word always brought a smile to her face. It was so deceptively deadly.

The rich sound of a horn rippled through the silence, causing all those waiting with Verre to glance up.

The prince had finally arrived.

Verre looked up as well, forcing an awed expression. It would not bode well for her if her disgust was evident.

There he was, descending the staircase. His unrestrained grandeur sickened her. His unicorn-fur robe alone could pay for an entire city's meals for one whole moon cycle! That, coupled with the fact that it was illegal to hunt unicorns, caused a spark of anger to burn deep inside Verre. Did no one care?

There was one thought that made Verre rather hopeful. She had heard rumors that the king had sired another child. It was obvious the king had many illegitimate children, considering his history, but none ever survived childhood.

Of course, it was merely speculation, but perhaps if the rumors were true, Allegora might regain some of its former glory, instead of just being known as the politically fragmented kingdom of Atulau.

As Verre glanced around, she saw shadows scurrying about, so slight she barely recognized them as humans. The king's many slaves, better known as handmaids and men. Of course, none of the other nobles noticed anything. Wealth was a wonderful blindfold to pain and suffering, and if Verre hadn't been brought up differently, she probably would be just like them.

Footsteps echoed, but Verre pointedly ignored them. A hand slithered along her shoulder, diverting her thought process. "And who might you be?" The slippery smoothness of the prince's voice nauseated Verre, but she retained her composure.

"Prince Jonad." She gave a curt bow and pulled away. "I am Lady Rira, the daughter of one of the eastern lords."

The prince gave her a curious look, and Verre wondered for a moment if he recognized her, but then she remembered her enchantment. Until the clock struck twelve, she would be unrecognizable. A witch had been quite helpful in enchanting the way she looked. Even if someone were to try and find Lady Rira, they would be disappointed to know she didn't even exist.

Prince Jonad's eyes raked over a woman to their left, Verre glancing over as well. Her dress was made of lace so fine it must have been created by the great spiders of the mountains. Definitely a pricey choice.

Of course, she doubted Jonad was inspecting the dress but rather what it didn't cover.

Averting her gaze, she studied him. If one were to go only on looks, he seemed like a pleasant enough man, especially with his splendid physique, deep brown eyes, and charming grin. But while his eyes were pretty, they had the look of a predator about them.

"Are you enjoying yourself tonight?" His mouth formed a subtle, pleased grin. At her brief nod, he continued, "Have you had a chance to see the palace gardens? They are unparalleled."

A garden. Secluded. Private. Alone. That was how it had happened to past women.

Fear wormed its way through Verre though she tried to placate it. He could do nothing to her. She was practically his height and just as strong. Still, the intensity with which he stared at her—his gaze occasionally drifting to the rest of her body—spoke volumes. Now

Verre understood to a small extent the terror Lora, the woman who had hired her, had been forced to experience.

She plastered a coy grin onto her face and placed a hand on his arm. "I would be honored, my prince."

"Then let us head there right away! I'll order some of the servants to bring food and drink there for us." The pleased expression on his face sent a shudder rushing down her spine. He guided her into the garden, his hand resting confidently on her hip.

"What is your favorite flower, Prince Jonad?" Verre asked as she inspected them closely, knowing that she'd never have another opportunity to see the rare beauties the palace was famous for. There was the dragon's heart, deep red flowers that bled in autumn; the moon blossoms, which were bright enough to be used as a source of light; and Verre's favorite, the angel's death, an innocent-looking white flower that had enough poison to kill even the most powerful of beings.

Deceptively deadly.

This simple thought helped relax her. She was a trained and conditioned killer. He could do nothing to her that she didn't allow. Besides, this was a mission to avenge.

"Unicorn tear has always been a personal favorite." Prince Jonad glanced at the cluster of glowing, purple buds that were surrounded by a shimmering gold shield.

Of course it would be unicorn tear. The flower only grew when a unicorn tear fell on fertile soil. Unicorns rarely shed tears, and the conditions had to be just right in order for the plant to thrive. Because of their ability to grant one wish, the unicorn tear was highly sought after.

Verre had heard rumors of how the royal family had managed to grow the entire cluster, of the unicorns they had tortured and the mages they had forced to create the perfect conditions for it to thrive.

"Unicorn tear? How incredibly rare. One hasn't been found in the wild in over a millennium." Verre turned from inspecting the angel's death to smile sweetly at Prince Jonad. "I'm surprised you were able to grow such a large amount, especially with the decrease in the unicorn population." She hoped the question seemed like one a dumb noblewoman would ask, though she was curious if he'd actually confess to never abiding by the own rules his family had set in place for the people of Allegora.

"Ah, sly, aren't we?" He smiled thinly. "I must say I'm hurt you wouldn't just come clean. Honestly, do you find me a fool?"

Verre frowned. "I can't begin to understand what you're trying to imply, my prince. Me? Sly? Never!" If he had discovered her deception, this mission might have to be messier than she wished.

He grinned, though it never reached his eyes. "Lady Rira! Do you mean to tell me that you didn't jump at the opportunity to see my gardens for the sole purpose of requesting a unicorn tear bud?"

Relief calmed her, and she flashed him a coy smile. "You've found me out, my prince. I was hoping to catch a glimpse of the famed flower and perhaps even ask for one. Who wouldn't?" Her fingers grabbed at a strand of hair that curled at her neck, watching how his gaze dropped to it immediately, his expression intense.

Then, searching her eyes, as if he didn't quite believe her, he nodded. "Of course." His hand trailed up her arm, his eyes never leaving hers. "Has this night been enjoyable?"

Gulping back nausea, she let his hand rest there. "Very much so. I had no idea the palace could host such elaborate parties." Her eyes left his to inspect the smooth marble of the palace itself, the glowing flowers casting odd shadows. The guests cast their own, twisting and swaying to the gentle music that flowed sweetly through the courtyards.

"Well, for being such pleasant company, Lady Rira, I'd like to offer you a room in the palace for the night. It would not do to have you sleeping in some inn."

Relief washed over Verre. The garden would have been far too public a place for a confrontation anyway. The prince could not have planned his own death any better. "Thank you for your kind offer, my dear prince. I am humbled." She bowed low, not even having to hide her delighted smile.

⸺⬥⸺

It was time.

She pulled on her usual trousers, having discarded the dress long before. The foolish prince had given her a room close to his own, something she was grateful for.

Verre slowly opened the door, her eyes widening at the prince's form standing right outside. Her breath caught, though her features remained frozen.

"Prince Jonad," she said softly. "What brings you here?"

"I think you know, dearest Rira," he said in a low voice, his eyes dark with greed as they swept over her. Putting a hand out to brush a strand of hair out of her face, he moved to enter the room.

"This is highly inappropriate! Remove yourself from my room, Your Majesty, or I will call the guards!" Verre allowed her voice to rise to a shrill squeak, enjoying the panic that lingered on his face.

It was replaced almost immediately with anger, his eyes so full of rage that chilling fear rushed through her. He reached out to grab her, but she was too fast. Grabbing his arm and stepping to the side, she snapped it, relishing his cry of pain far more than she would have thought.

He recovered quickly, though, bringing a perfectly healthy fist crashing into her jaw. The pain did little but enrage her. "Who are you?" he demanded, slowly inching toward her. His mistake.

Verre slipped by him, shutting the door and effectively trapping Jonad in the bedroom with her. There was no hope for him now. His brows furrowed in confusion.

Glass formed in her clenched fist, a long shard, wickedly sharp. She shoved it into his thigh, causing him to cry out in pain.

The image of a defenseless woman, pleading with the prince came to mind, filling her with the rage she needed.

"Does that hurt?" She clicked her tongue in a disapproving way, ramming another shard into his right shoulder.

A low moan of pain.

"Lora sends her regards," Verre whispered in his ear before sending one last shard through his gut.

She tossed the blood-stained prince to the ground, glancing at the stains he'd left on her in disgust. He would have assaulted her too if he had been given the chance.

"How does it feel to be the victim?" she said softly, his eyes widening in realization. "No one to help you, no one to call for. Terrifying, right?" He said nothing, either the fear or pain having stilled his tongue.

Seeing him lying there, Verre forced herself to believe this was justice. Messy, yes, but necessary. Now he would no longer harm another woman.

"Can't leave any evidence, can we?" With a flick of her hand, the glass disappeared from his body, bloody wounds the only indication of a weapon.

Glass. How ironic that it was more deadly when broken than whole. And how Verre enjoyed her things broken.

The palace clock boomed. It was midnight. Verre's disguise melted away, restoring her tall, lithe figure, her hair tickling her jaw. Her eyes alighted on the prince's form. He was still alive

"Verre?" He whispered, blood bubbling over his lips, his breath coming in ragged gasps.

All the rage flickered out and like a punch to the gut, she realized she had gone too far. Verre might be a killer, but torture was never acceptable. Shaking her head to try and rid herself of these thoughts, she sent one last shard through his brain. Minimal pain, minimal suffering. "Goodbye, Jonad."

3

BLANCA

THE FIRST THING Blanca felt was cold. An icy cold that seeped into her bones. Opening her eyes slowly, she tried to take in her surroundings. Four walls… a room. A small one at that. It was cluttered with jars and bottles, and an odd, sharp smell filled the air, almost like a thousand different herbs had been crushed together.

Trying to sit up, Blanca realized that a bubble-like sphere was covering her face, siphoning some green mist into a glass jar nearby. Panic swelling, Blanca ripped it off, allowing it to flutter to the ground.

"Hello?" she croaked, her throat burning. A tendril of the green mist escaped her lips again, winding its way through the air. Blanca clamped a hand over her mouth. That wasn't normal. People didn't just breathe mist. And it was green. She shakily removed her hand once more, her labored breathing creating even more of the stuff.

A door opened, causing Blanca to jump, her nerves already wound tight.

A lone, elderly man entered, a similar bubble around his head. "Hello, m'dear. I'm relieved to see you awake; you've been asleep for quite some time." He sat himself down in a chair to her left, picking up the jar that still contained the green fog. "I must say, you've made this room extremely dangerous within the short time I left you unattended." His tone wasn't accusatory; instead, it was warm and pleasant as if they were old friends.

"Who are you?" Blanca whispered, her mouth on fire. But, as she thought about it, she didn't even know who she was. If her heart was beating rapidly before, it most definitely was going to explode now. She closed her eyes, trying to bring to mind anyone... anything.

"I am Randule, one of the High Mages. And you, m'dear, are a very special person indeed." He smiled warmly and placed the jar back down. "Please don't be frightened if you're not able to recall much. Our experiment seems to have made certain memories disappear, but I have confidence they will return within the next few weeks."

Blanca's mind swam with questions and confusion. "Why did you take my memories? And what," she stammered, "what is this mist?"

Randule's expression changed, the smile fading away. "Well, you see, I found you in a forest. And," his gaze fell from hers, finding the floor instead, "you were dead. I didn't learn of the poison until after you were brought back."

She had died? Her head ached, and her throat wouldn't stop hurting. Her heart thudded rapidly against her chest. Why couldn't it stop pounding? Blanca didn't realize she was falling off the edge of her bed until she hit the floor.

———❖———

Blanca carefully opened her eyes, a sense of déjà vu overwhelming her. Same room, same jars, same mist hovering around her face. Except it now had a name. Poison. A shudder swept through her and the man sitting next to her turned. Randule. At least she knew that much.

"My apologies," he stated slowly. "I hadn't thought how the news might affect you, especially with no memories. This all must be too much."

What was she supposed to say? Her brain couldn't form a full thought or question without bringing on a headache. She could feel one brewing now.

Randule seemed to understand, for his expression softened. "In pain? I can offer something for that. I wish I could offer some advice too, but bringing someone back from the dead… It is forbidden magic and extremely difficult to wield."

"Why did you do it then? If it is forbidden, then why disobey the king?" Talking felt like she was trying to shout through a door, every word a chore.

"The king?" He looked surprised. "You remember him? How odd. Well, King Jore has many flawed concepts of how a country should be run. I'm not overly fond of him, if you get my meaning. When I saw you alone in the forest, it reminded me of my own daughter. She's away studying in Moorehaven—such a beautiful kingdom—but I couldn't shake the feeling she would be disappointed in me if I didn't at least try to bring you back."

So Randule didn't agree with the king. That was treason. For some reason, that made Blanca angry. The king knew best, even if she had only vague memories of him. It wasn't the mage's place to defy or question him. "What you did was wrong."

His eyes narrowed slightly at her comment. "Perhaps, but you are alive once more, though a bit deadlier than before." He rose from his seat, coming over to adjust her air bubble.

She shrank away, the action triggering a deep-seated fear for some reason. Her body trembled as his fingers brushed her neck while he finished adjusting the bubble. "There," he said cheerfully. "No stray poison will be escaping."

He grabbed a vial beside her and swirled it gently. The grey color wasn't appealing, and when he handed it to her to drink, she recoiled. Who knew what was in it?

"For the pain," he explained.

Tentatively, she grabbed the vial and held it up to the bubble, pushing through it with surprising ease. The poison didn't escape, though. Taking a sip, she was surprised by the immediate effects. The pain disappeared, leaving her with a pleasant numbness.

"Now," Randule continued, "how about we try and spark some memories? That potion should help bring some back, though they may be scattered and a bit confusing."

Closing her eyes, she tried to bring order to the random images that were never in focus and just out of grasp. Surprisingly, it worked.

"Lyra," Blanca whispered. For some reason, the name brought a memory of cold. Snowflakes were falling in a silent forest. There was laughter and a bright blue dress. The name made Blanca want to smile, though the face accompanying the name was nothing but a hazy blur.

"Lyra?" Randule's brows furrowed in thought. "The name is oddly familiar." He rose and consulted a glowing sphere that was floating above a golden pedestal. An image rippled into view. A dark-haired woman was smiling, her high cheekbones and red, laughing mouth only a small indication of the woman's exquisite beauty.

Blanca grimaced, the face triggering a series of images.

"Hurry up, Blanca!" the young woman shouted, her shimmering blue gown catching the light reflected upon the fresh snow. Her dark hair was flowing down her back, her ivory skin flushed in the cold. Blanca had never seen a more beautiful woman than her youthful stepmother and believed she never would.

"I'm hurrying!" she shouted playfully back, trying to wade through the ankle-deep snow in her own gown of gold.

"We're going to be late," Lyra protested, her full lips forming a pout. Blanca had always secretly thought of herself as the more mature of the two though Lyra was ten years older. Lyra was far too young to be her father's bride, her twenty-five years a stark contrast to his forty-three. But Lyra never complained though Blanca knew she'd had no say in the matter.

"You exaggerate far too often, Lyra," Blanca laughed and ran to catch up, her breath coming in ragged gasps as she slowed down next to Lyra.

"I know." Lyra's eyes twinkled.

After struggling for a few more minutes in the snow, they came upon a clearing, the source of their search. "Look," whispered Lyra, her eyes shining. "Isn't it beautiful?"

Blanca's eyes widened at the sight below. Four dryads danced in the clearing, each movement like the faintest trace of a breeze as it caressed a tree's branches. In the center of the clearing, a lone, young tree stood, its branches naked. The dryads were speaking softly to it, their voices no louder than the tinkling of a bell but all the sweeter.

Slowly, as if drawn by their coaxing song, a slender arm reached through the rough bark, a small head clad in brown curls following. Two doe-like eyes blinked in astonishment at the world around them. The dryads enveloped the new young dryad in their arms, their song one of thankfulness and joy.

"Oh my," breathed Blanca, turning to glance at Lyra. The birth of a dryad was truly a rare occasion, one that only happened during the eve of spring at a certain time of day.

"It was indeed beautiful." Lyra hesitated, her eyes conveying uncertainty. "Blanca? I have something I must tell you." Her hands rested on her stomach, a mixture of fear and excitement caused a small grin to form on her face. "I am expecting."

Expecting?

Realization dawned on Blanca, and she hugged Lyra tight. "A child? Why, Lyra, this is magnificent!" The words were a mite too loud, and the dryads melded into the trees, gone in but a moment.

"You're not upset? I was afraid this might ruin our fun times." Lyra smiled in relief. "I believe it might be fun, having a wee little one following us about and perhaps seeing the birth of a dryad as well."

"This is splendid," Blanca said. "We shall have even more fun, the three of us. But what about Father? Does he know?" Speaking his name caused a chill to settle in Blanca's bones. He was not a kind man nor a loving one. Blanca tried to believe that his heart was cold because the love of his life—Blanca's dear mother—had passed on, but Blanca knew better. He was simply a cruel man who could not even love his own flesh and blood.

"I have not told him, not yet. You know how your father gets. I'm afraid he'll go into a rage and throw things as he usually does. But I'm hoping he'll be excited. Perhaps having another child will do him good." Lyra bit her lip, knowing that the hope was a vain one. Blanca's father loved only one thing: his title.

Lord Rikor had been a good man at one point, before his title and the incident that took his wife's life. Every time he returned from discussions with the king, he came back sterner, fiercer, and with a tendency to drink his worries away. Now that man, the one Blanca had loved and cherished, wasn't going to come back, no matter how much she wished for him to.

"I'm sure it will all be perfectly fine," Blanca said, holding Lyra close, feeling the tenseness of her body. It had to be fine.

"Lyra," Blanca whispered again, tears pooling in her eyes. The one memory was so strong, she could nearly feel the cold snow around her. She clutched at any other memories of Lyra but remembered nothing. What of the child? Her father? The name still made her shudder, and she could feel that her memories of him were not pleasant in the slightest.

Randule approached her once more, his countenance sorrowful. "I'm sorry that was so painful, Blanca. Though it seems to have been somewhat pleasant, correct? I have heard much of your father, Lord Rikor of Ebeni. A powerful man indeed."

Lord Rikor. The name brought a sense of dread, but Blanca refused to allow herself to associate any memories with it, not yet. The nearness of the first memory faded, but it was still there, lingering in the back of her mind. Blanca held onto it, savoring the pure joy it sent rushing through her.

And her name—Blanca. How sweet it had sounded coming from Lyra's mouth. It had sounded loved and wanted. She desperately needed that back, no matter what.

4

AURA

THERE IT WAS. Aura licked her lips as she stared hungrily into the window. The peak perfection of a delicacy. The golden standard of food. A meat pie. And it was about to be hers.

Rising slowly from where she was crouched behind a crate, she made her way over to the small bakery. The heavy scent of meat accompanied by the light sweetness of bread was enough to make her drool. It had been days since she'd had a proper meal.

Combing her greasy hair back into a serviceable bun, Aura crossed the noisy street, making last-minute adjustments to her grey, mud-stained dress. Countless carriages rumbled by, and hooded men stood at every corner, but Aura was skilled at surviving the streets of Oobay.

The city was known for its high mortality rate and terrible living conditions. Children were taken from parents daily to either slave in the mines and factories, or worse, serve the king. Aura had managed to stay alive and free—being a sixteen-year-old girl was incredibly rare in Oobay—but she had the Ancient Ones and possibly her heritage to thank for that.

"Hey, you!" One of the king's hooded men stepped forward. "What is your occupation?"

Aura strode confidently over to him, having done this countless times before, though the slight quiver of her limbs never went away. "I work at the wand factory just a few streets from here."

She hoped her slight frame wouldn't give away her age. Women over the age of twenty were mostly ignored; it was those who were between the ages of thirteen and nineteen that were in danger of being taken.

"Huh, parents are gone?" The man removed a scroll from his cloak and unrolled it. "Just need your name so I can see if your story is true." He grinned slowly. "What a pity it'd be if it isn't."

Aura swore silently; a scroll definitely changed things. The mages had crafted them for the use of the Guardsmen—the hooded ones. The scrolls could read minds, but permission needed to be given first in the form of the person's name. Very few would die rather than give their name, but Aura most definitely would.

"My name?" Aura closed her eyes, allowing herself to feel the pulsing mind of the hooded one in front of her. There was always something off about their minds, a void to them.

Ignoring the ominous thought, she allowed herself to probe his mind, instilling a command of sleep. A thud was all she needed to break from her concentration.

Her eyes opened, and a slow smirk formed on her face. There he was, collapsed on the ground, stuck in a deep sleep. He would wake in a few minutes—her touch was more potent—but it was enough time to escape. Glancing around quickly, she noted that there were only about four people who could have possibly seen her. Given the fact that one was too little to know what he saw and the others were too occupied with their stroll to work, she risked not creating a fake scene.

Fighting the urge to steal the scroll only Guardsmen could use, she moved on to her initial target, the bakery. The door swung open, a merry tinkling of a bell following. The aroma of so much fresh food nearly made Aura collapse in hunger. Forcing slumber on the hooded one had drained her, and she was already malnourished. But she still had the energy for one more command.

"Can I help ye?" An older man—perhaps thirty—stepped out from a wooden doorway, his short brown beard dusted in flour. He was tall, much taller than Aura, but she didn't have to fear him.

"I was wondering how much your meat pies are?" Her deep, raspy voice seemed to surprise the older man, but it was expected. She was just five feet with the frame of a wooden rail.

"Three ha'silvers per pie. Loaves are but a copper. Ye sure ye have the coin for a pie?" The man's accent was peculiar, similar to the miners of the Bluefrost mountains. Aura had never been outside of Oobay, but she'd always dreamed of traveling Allegora.

Taking a quick look around, she said, "I'm afraid I don't." Aura snatched the man's arm, projecting sleep as strongly as she could. He tumbled to the ground, a confused expression on his face. Snatching two meat pies, Aura raced out the back door, glancing in pity at the man. "I'm sorry," she whispered before hurrying out into the smoky alley.

"Look what I have!" Aura crawled through the entrance to their makeshift home—more a shack made of a bunch of stacked crates and mildewy blankets, but a home nonetheless. Two dirty little faces popped up from the mass of rags in the corner, materializing into two young bodies.

"Aura!" squealed Aela, the youngest of the three. "Have any food?" Aerik scrambled over as well, his eyes wide with delight. "What is that smell!"

Aura put a finger to her lips, her face stern, but her eyes crinkling at the corners. "I have two meat pies to share, but you have to be quiet. If others were to hear you, who knows what they'd do."

The two little ones nodded seriously, shifting nervously at the thought. Their home alley was a dangerous one, though among the nicest in Oobay, if that counted for anything. If it weren't for Aura's reputation of silencing even the most deadly, the three of them would have been killed already, or worse, sold.

"Can we eat them now?" little Aela asked, her eyes hopeful. She was small, even for the age of eight. Her ribs showed through the thin rag of a dress that encompassed her body. If Aura and Aerik were underweight, then Aela was emaciated.

Caring for them was difficult, especially since Aura refused to work in the factories. They caused far too much death, and Aela and Aerik couldn't lose her too.

Their father had been sentenced to work in the mines after stealing some medicine Aela had needed. No one ever returned from the mines. And her mother… Aura glanced down at the meat pies in her hands and closed her eyes at the memory. The hooded ones had taken her to serve the king, and she had never come back. Families were a hopeless dream in Oobay, as were many things.

"Aura? Are you listening? We want food!" Aerik's loud whine brought her back to the present. Her siblings were practically drooling with hunger.

"Shh, of course! I'm sorry, I was just… remembering." Aura smiled and placed one of the meat pies on the crate that served as a table. Aela had tried to make it look like a real table with a plaid piece of cloth that had long since lost its vibrant hues. "Eat slowly, understand? This meat pie is good for you, but it's a bit rich. We'll save as much as we can."

The two nodded and began to dig in, but were stopped by Aura. "Not with such dirty hands! Do you want to get sick? Go on, hurry and wash them." She grinned and shooed them to the far corner of their small home. A leaking pipe ran along the side of the building next to them. They had a cracked pot propped up underneath it, so as to not waste any of the precious water.

Cupping their hands underneath the steady drip, they were soon done, their faces and hands glistening wet. "We have no clean cloths, so just shake them dry." Aura shook her hands vigorously, laughing as Aela shook so hard that she fell down.

"Ready to eat now?" A hearty yes followed.

Sitting down, they all dug in, humming in satisfaction as the flaky crust revealed tender meat, rich gravy, and bright green vegetables.

The first pie was devoured in a matter of minutes despite Aura's warning, which she ignored herself. "We're saving the second one until tomorrow; is that understood? We can't afford to eat two in one day."

Aela sighed in disappointment. "I could eat a whole dragon. I'm still so hungry." She patted her little stomach sadly.

"That pie was good." Aerik nodded in agreement. "Best one I've ever eaten."

Aura laughed and pulled them into a hug. "Let your stomach sit a little; I'm sure you'll feel full in a few minutes. Though I feel like I could eat a whole dragon too."

Aerik pulled away slightly, his expression thoughtful. "If I were to find a dragon and tame it, teaching it to listen to me, we could fly away from here." His voice rose in excitement. "We could go live in the mountains, or maybe the forest. If we had a dragon, you could finally travel all over Atulau like you've always wanted to, Aura."

She blinked away tears and smiled, drawing them close again. "If you were ever to find a dragon, Aerik, I have no doubt it would learn to love you and trust you. But I don't need a dragon to see the world. I have my whole world with me right here."

Aela snuggled up against her, her deep brown eyes wistful. "If I had to choose a dragon or you, I'd choose you. But I still would like to see a forest. I hear they're big and green, and the trees go this high." She gestured with her arms, trying to throw them as wide as possible. "Do you think we'll see a real tree someday? The ones here are tiny, and they never have any pretty leaves."

Aura nodded. "Yes, someday you'll see a real tree. I promise."

5

CERISE

CERISE CROUCHED IN the tree, her eyes taking in the forest floor that spread out below her. It had been thirty hours since she had last eaten, and every fiber in her body screamed to be fed. Normally it was all too easy to find food, but that was when she had been living with Raina and the ax that she had lent her had become a third arm. But both Raina and the ax were gone, and only Cerise and the wolf remained.

The wolf begged to be let free, to kill something and be satisfied with fresh meat, but Cerise refused. She knew what happened when she wasn't able to retain control.

At first, it hadn't been too much trouble finding food in her human form. There were fish in the underground river, which Cerise could catch with relative ease. But it had been a week since the fish had gone. Either they had moved on or Cerise had eaten them all.

Then had come the frogs and worms that were hiding in the crevasses of the dark passageways. But those, too, were scarce now. It was time to hunt.

Cerise gripped the wooden spear tightly as she waited, hoping some unfortunate creature would come her way, preferably a hark.

The creatures were small and plump, usually roosting in the eaves of old buildings and speeding along on the ground. Their nasty little teeth could leave an infection, but fortunately, they were stupid and quite delicious when cooked right.

Her stomach growled at the thought. Hark was actually a staple food in most of the homes in Lithrium. They were relatively easy to catch, and they bred quickly. If hark wasn't eaten by many of the creatures within the forest and the surrounding villages, they would overrun everything.

Thinking of her village made Cerise's heart wrench. She used to consider it her home. Back when people didn't know she was a hybrid, of course. She had seen over and over what Allegorians did to rogue magic-wielders, especially hybrids. Public executions were far too common, and Cerise had been forced to witness far too many. Only the mages and well-behaved witches were accepted.

The soft crumble of decaying leaves caused Cerise to tense and glance in the direction of the sound. Whatever it was, it wasn't very large and came her way at a leisurely pace. It had not scented her yet.

Her stance shifted slightly, preparing her for the leap to the ground. She adjusted her grip on the spear softly, trying to make as little noise as possible. Another crackle, this time closer. A smile slowly formed on her face. Perhaps it was a hark after all. She could almost picture the creature now, skinned and roasting over an open fire. The juices dripping into the flames below...

A soft hiss sounded directly beneath her, nearly making her lose her grip on the spear. The hark hopped below, rooting its long snout in the loose soil at the base of the tree, no doubt looking for grubs.

Instinct took over, her body morphing as she leapt from the tree. Strong legs hit the ground, her claws digging into the soft dirt. The hark squeaked in surprise, scurrying away. The wolf's maw dripped saliva as she easily chased after the creature. Muscles tense, she jumped, bringing her jaws around the hark's neck, snapping it cleanly.

Dropping it, the wolf let out a happy bark, the taste of blood driving her crazy. But she didn't eat the hark. She had to cook it first. The thought brought Cerise's conscious racing to the front of her brain.

Had she really shifted that quickly? Cerise sat on her haunches, too shocked by being herself in the wolf's body to eat.

Rising, she trembled as she felt the wild strength in her limbs, the sharp teeth stained with blood. She hated this. Hated being an animal.

The sharp scent of blood brought her thoughts back to her hunger. She didn't want to just eat it. It would taste so much better if she cooked it, but that would require the tricky task of shifting back.

It couldn't be that hard, right? In just the past week, she'd had to shift multiple times. She was far from perfecting it, but it shouldn't be too difficult now.

She focused on her body, feeling the new muscles, the fur, the claws. She pictured her human form, the smooth skin, the feet, and her curly hair. She willed her body to morph, to simply switch.

The familiar pain, the stretching of skin, the curling of her stomach too. It was working.

Cerise rose from the ground, quickly walking to where her torn clothes had been abandoned. They were still wearable, so she pulled them on, her hunger no longer able to be ignored. She licked a drop of blood from the corner of her mouth, surprised to enjoy the taste.

───────◆───────

The fire crackled softly, tendrils reaching toward the sky. Cerise watched as the flesh of the hark browned, bringing with it the most tantalizing of smells. She had foraged for some wild onions and bitteroot, a surprisingly delicious seasoning, and stuffed them into the gutted carcass of the hark.

It was nearly nightfall, and the shadows of the trees were fading. Cooking out in the open was dangerous, but creating a fire in her cave network was as well. She would have to be quick before other creatures followed the scent of the food—creatures that were much more frightening than a hark.

The meat popped, and Cerise tensed at the break in silence. The fast-growing darkness made her uneasy; nothing good ever happened in the forest of Lithrium at night.

Removing the stick the hark had been driven on—and nearly dropping it from the heat—Cerise tore into it, the juices running freely down her face. The roasted hark was almost too hot, but Cerise was too hungry to care. Picked to the bone within minutes, Cerise vainly tried to suck the last sweet drops from each. Who knew when she'd eat this well again?

Wiping her greasy face on the sleeve of her blouse, Cerise rose and threw dirt on the fire to put it out. The fire sputtered in an attempt to stay alight but was quickly smothered. If there was anything Cerise had learned while living in the forest, it was the fact that fire might just be the most deadly enemy of all.

Darkness had consumed the forest. Once the fire had been put out, it became even more evident how late it was. Full and happy, Cerise did not mind the walk back to her caves, especially not with a spear in hand. Her clothes were filthy, though, and Cerise made a note to wash them once she had safely returned to her cave.

A sound reached her ears and she froze; her ears strained to figure out what it could be. Footsteps. The noise was footsteps. Her heartbeat pulsed rapidly through her body. Whoever it was, they were an expert, melting into the shadows whenever she casually glanced around. They were stealthy too. Cerise only heard them every few minutes, far too infrequently for comfort. It was not a villager, and it certainly wasn't a trigor. Whoever—or perhaps, whatever—it was, they were dangerous.

Cerise picked up her pace, rewarded with more footsteps, a tad clumsier this time. Still, it took all of her hearing to pick up on the sound. She was never going to make it to the caves without a confrontation. The element of surprise was still on her side. Perhaps she could catch them off-guard.

Taking a steadying breath, she melded with the shadows, choosing where to step carefully. She needed to shift. Confident from her last experience, she allowed her body to change once more, the pain dull compared to past times.

The hard eyes of the large brown wolf scanned the forest, picking out a humanoid figure to her left. It appeared to be a man, and it also appeared confused. Crouching low, the wolf stalked the man, soon classifying him with a scent. Now she'd be able to track him.

He was only one lunge away. She could hear his heart beating calmly, his scent heavy around him. He wasn't panicking? Then the man disappeared.

The wolf backed away in surprise. His scent was still there, just… faint. As if he had moved. But how was that possible?

A low chuckle sounded behind her. The wolf snarled and snapped, leaving a bloody gash in the man's arm. He didn't even flinch, just stood in amazement as the blood dripped down his arm. "I must say, I didn't expect you to be so difficult to find, or to capture. I most certainly didn't believe you'd be able to draw blood." His voice was deep but icy cold.

The wolf backed up, unable to process what was happening. The man's skin was closing shut, the wound gone. She snarled again, a warning to keep his distance.

He paid her no mind, pulling a sword out of a sheath across his back. "Please don't fight. Madame Rose will be so disappointed if I hurt one of her toys. But I *will* hurt you if necessary. Don't test me, little wolf."

The wolf whined softly at the fear that welled up inside of her. No one should be able to just heal, especially after a bite like that.

Darting into the brush, she used her agile body to disappear, watching him from a distance. The man vanished again. The wolf whirled all around, her heart pounding irregularly. His scent surrounded her, but she couldn't find him. A small whimper escaped her throat. She knew she was outmatched.

"What a smart but hopeless ploy, my dear little wolf."

She turned to attack, but it was too late. He brought his sword pommel crashing down on her skull. Pain rippled through the wolf as she tried to stay upright, but blackness tore at the edges of her vision, eventually stealing her mind completely.

VERRE

"I'M BACK," VERRE called out, stepping into the ornate room filled with artwork and potted plants. It would have been perfectly normal except for the fact that the numerous pots and plants were lazily floating and moving about overhead. Simply an adorable quirk of her mother's until someone smacked their face on one.

Verre smiled fondly; she was home. "Hello? Anyone here?"

A matronly woman appeared from around the corner, dirt smudged on her face and gown. It was a beautiful dress with silk embroidery and a rich green satin material. But it was now filthy and had little tears. There was even a stray rose branch tangled in her dark hair.

"Verre! I wasn't expecting you back so soon. Your father is busy at the moment, you know him, always studying in that library of his." Her mother rolled her eyes, but Verre could see the twinkle she tried to conceal.

"You've been married thirty years now, Mother. You really expect me to believe that Father's bookish ways are a nuisance?" Verre jabbed her mother playfully, earning a smack in return.

"Ah, you saucy girl. I've half a mind to deprive you of supper like I used to do when you'd sass me." Her mother folded her arms across her ample chest and frowned. If Verre didn't know her mother, she would have actually believed her to be angry.

"But you won't," Verre smirked and kissed Mother's cheek. "Have you seen Baen? He hasn't tried to contact me at all." Baen was her husband, and they had celebrated two years of marriage just a month ago. While sometimes it still felt like a dream to Verre, she'd never regretted it.

"He's upstairs. Been busy all day creating a new water pot for me. He says this one will be able to hold twice as much and not spill half like the last one had a tendency to," Mother said.

Everyone in her family had their oddities. In fact, they were known for them. Mother, the botanist; Father, the scholar; Baen, the inventor. But then there was Verre, whose only talent seemed to be killing people for a living. But it was best to not dwell on that fact. Verre had learned early on that negative thoughts were best taken care of when they were closed up in a small corner of her brain.

Her parents were the Lord and Lady of Berth. The people of Berth loved them, for while her parents could be a tad absent-minded, they were good and kind, and their people prospered.

Verre often wondered how they'd gotten such a child as her—an assassin of all things. She had always had a fascination with knives even before she learned of her ability. While her parents were hesitant to even eat hark, Verre had no problems killing, so long as it was for the right reasons.

"Ice Princess, darling! I can't believe you're home so soon. Are you allowed to tell us where you've been? Or is that forbidden?" Baen slid down the banister and kissed Verre full on the mouth.

A chuckle bubbled up her throat. "Jester! I'm disappointed you didn't come to welcome me home sooner! It's not like you love me or anything, right?" She grinned and wrapped her arms around his neck, relaxing in the warmth and happiness of being home.

Sometimes it felt like she led two completely different lives: the one with her family and the one where she did everything alone. One was a pleasure, and one was a necessity.

He slid his hands around her waist, drawing her close. "I sincerely apologize. Do you forgive me?" His pleading brown eyes were too much for Verre to resist. That and his adorable dimple that only appeared when he genuinely smiled…

"Fine, you are forgiven, but only this one time." She gave him one last kiss and pulled away. "I'm starving. Mother, do you have anything for your poor daughter?"

Her mother stood to the side, her arms crossed, a real frown on her face. Her parents were unaware of her 'real' occupation. They thought she was a member of the king's army, a man both her parents strongly disapproved of. They knew Verre hated the monarchy and thought that she did it simply to get close enough to the king to finally dispatch him. While her parents might hate the king as well, they didn't condone killing him. Just wait till news of Jonad's death arrived… But she had a good day or two before that required an explanation.

"Is this about my career choice? Mother, we've discussed this." They had discussed it many times, and it stood as the only thing she did that her parents genuinely disapproved of.

Her mother huffed. "I know, dear. You're a grown woman and can make your own decisions, but you know how I feel on the matter." She brushed her hands off on her skirt briskly. "I might have some fresh rolls and hot soup if you can bring yourself to give your dear old mother a hug and a kiss."

Rolling her eyes, Verre gave her mother a quick kiss, whirling a shard of glass carelessly in her fingers.

"Verre!" she whispered sharply, eyes wide with fear. "Put that thing away! If the king ever found out…"

"There's no need to worry, Mother. He'll never find out." Her mother's fears weren't unwarranted, though. If King Jore ever did find out that one of the wealthiest noblewomen was an unapproved magic-wielder… Well, they'd probably all be decapitated in their sleep.

Wanting to end the conversation before it got even more serious, Verre gave her frowning mother a quick hug before hurrying to their large kitchen. They had servants for the cooking and cleaning, but her mother preferred to do most of it herself, saying it made it feel more like a home. To be a servant at Berth Manor was the highest honor. The servants were treated practically like family and paid generously for their work.

A pair of hands stole about her waist, snatching one of her rolls. "How long are you home? Will I have to lay awake at night mourning the loss of my beloved so soon?"

Verre rolled her eyes and continued eating. There he went again, being dramatic. Perhaps he could learn from her that emotions should be controlled and released only when you wished them to.

"Darling, do you not hear my tale of woe?"

She sighed and turned, snatching the roll back. "I heard indeed, but I chose to ignore it." She took a bite out of her roll, grinning as his face fell. It would do him good to be ignored every once in a while. She didn't need a conceited husband; Baen was conceited enough already.

"Do you know what I need? I need a good massage for my back, perhaps my feet as well. I'm quite sore and in need of relaxation. So to answer your question, beloved, I will be staying home for a while."

"If you're in need of rest, then I will make sure the servants draw a bath at once. Nothing is too good for you, darling. And who knows? Maybe as I massage you we can *finally* discuss that trip to Evanscene? The elves are among the best metal workers in all of Atulau, you know, but I'll go draw that bath now." He scrambled up after placing a quick kiss to her temple and was gone in moments.

Verre watched him leave with a twinge of regret. It had been months since they last spent some actual time together, hence his seventh request that year to travel. That and the fact that Baen was a born adventurer.

Her parents had offered them the titles as Lord and Lady of Berth, but they didn't feel equipped for that kind of responsibility. So Baen pursued his dream and Verre... She did the only thing she was good at.

Thankfully, hired assassins made more than one would imagine as there was always some nobleman who was willing to pay much coin to have a rival conveniently eliminated. And there was nothing Verre liked more than rebelling against Allegora's miserable excuse for a ruler, King Jore, and his cohorts.

In Lora's case, it had been worth it simply to know that Jonad would no longer torment her world. Besides, the woman would never have been able to pay her, though she did provide Verre with all the enchantments and equipment necessary. But thinking back to the mission... She had killed the heir to Allegora. The thought sent chills coursing across her skin.

The image of him on the ground bleeding crept unbidden in her mind. He had deserved it, she reminded herself yet again. She had to learn to make peace with who she had become. Sometimes you had to be a monster so no one else had to. And sometimes only a monster could defeat another monster.

She took a bite of her roll, desperate for a distraction. When her gifts had first been discovered, she had vowed to only use them for the good of the common people. Where she drew the line was not quite as defined as it used to be, but she was willing to sacrifice her innocence for the people of Allegora.

Sighing, Verre stuffed in the last of the roll and stumbled up to her rooms, far more exhausted than she had let on. Settling onto the down feather mattress, she allowed herself to close off from her drained emotions.

It was her daily routine, right before she retired for the night. Verre didn't handle emotion well, always forcing herself to appear detached. Except around her family.

"Reposing? My, my, I never expected Allegora's most elite assassin to be so calm and tranquil after such a gruesome murder, but perhaps that's what makes you the best." The voice was silky smooth, yet deep and cold, tinged with a dark amusement that wound its way around Verre's heart.

She jumped up and whirled smoothly, a shard of glass penetrating deep within the man's chest. His dark eyes danced with a cold light, and his body melted into shadows, reappearing to her right. Dark realization hit her. He must have used this strange power to get in her room.

"That's the second time I've bled this past week," the man said. "I must say, my dignity has been injured." He pulled the shard out, its tip blackened with blood. As Verre watched, the wound quickly closed, no hint of a scar remaining.

Verre ran through every magic-wielder she had ever encountered, but none had healing capabilities like that. He knew about her too, so had someone tipped him off? But who?

She constructed a wall of glass, sending it charging toward the man. With her other hand, she sent a cluster of shards directly at his head. He dodged the shards and simply disappeared once more to avoid the shield.

Verre crouched low to the ground, her weariness forgotten. Had some of her enemies finally sent an assassin of their own? But how had they found her?

Pushing these thoughts aside, Verre sent another volley of shards, then rose up another sheet of glass underneath him. The man's eyes widened as his legs gave out beneath him, his forehead catching the edge of a lampstand. Verre slashed his cheek open to the bone, pinning him to the ground. For the first time, he appeared to be in pain.

"Who are you?" Verre finally asked.

He grinned, enveloping them both in shadows. Verre tried to scramble away, but it was too late. The world went cold and dark, wispy images and gasps of cold breath whispering by, raising goosebumps on her flesh. Everything was silent, so much so that she could hear her own blood pumping wildly through her veins. Suddenly there was a rush of light, and they were back. Wherever back was.

Whoever this man was, he was deadly and could not be trusted. His abilities were both strange and terrifying. Fear—that was an emotion Verre was not accustomed to.

She staggered upright, trying to take inventory of everything around her. All she managed was a quick glimpse of a garden before her eyes went dark. With the smell of lavender permeating the air, Verre knew it could only be one thing. Narco powder. It was a favorite of the Guardsmen, who used it to blind their enemies temporarily. Verre had used it before herself.

"Hello, m'dear," a lilting voice called, sickeningly sweet. "I'm so glad you could join us."

BLANCA

HE WAS SCREAMING *again. Blanca tried to block out his voice by cupping her hands over her ears, but it always managed to worm its way through, invading her mind. Usually, Lyra could appease him, but it had become increasingly difficult. Ever since baby Rose had been born, the man had become more and more aggressive, often throwing things. He spent time with the king almost every day; her father was only ever home to hurt them.*

He had a new gift from the king, too—a mirror. But it wasn't an ordinary mirror, for Blanca had heard it talk to her father on more than one occasion. It was magic, and her father was obsessed with it.

She still remembered the humiliation of standing in front of it as her father chanted "Mirror, mirror on the wall: who is the fairest of them all?" She also remembered how painful a shattered wine bottle felt when it burrowed deep into your arm. If only she was the fairest... maybe he'd finally be content.

"Blanca?" The soft whisper almost went unnoticed through the screaming. She opened her eyes slowly, Lyra's pensive face coming into focus. "I need you to take Rose outside for a walk. Your father…" Lyra's voice trembled. "He's worse than usual. Marcos is half-dead because of something he said. I'm afraid of what he might do to the two of you. I need you to pack a satchel of clothing and necessities and leave. Don't come back unless you see a bouquet of bitteroot in the archway of the manor. Is that understood? I've set aside some coin as well; spend it sparingly." She handed the flushed infant to Blanca, along with a purse of coins and a look full of trust that said this was no walk.

Blanca closed her eyes, exhaling softly. "Why don't you join us? We could escape together and never come back. He wouldn't be able to find us." Blanca's throat was bone-dry with fear, her stomach trying to squirm its way up and out of her mouth. Her father was a monster, and she would be overjoyed to never have to look into his cruel eyes for the rest of her days.

Lyra sighed, tears forming in her eyes and winding their way down her cheeks. "It's complicated. According to the law set in place by King Jore, I'm not legally allowed to leave your father's home unless we can definitively prove his abuse toward us. We would have to petition the king, and you know how close they are. If I sneak you two away and remain myself, I can appease your father. I'm sure in time it will be safe to return. This can't last forever, right?"

The quivering smile on Lyra's face tore at Blanca's heart. It was such a painfully hopeful lie. She was seventeen now and knew all too well how horrific her *home had grown. The law would indeed rule in favor of her father, and they'd only end up provoking him further. Lyra was making a sacrifice, and Blanca needed to make sure Rose would be safe. "I understand. We must protect Rose."*

Lyra nodded slowly, trembling, though she tried to conceal it. "As long as you two escape, I will be happy. I will try to find a way to keep in touch without your father finding out—perhaps a trustworthy servant? But no matter, you must hurry! He will be searching for me presently. Go!" She shoved them along toward Blanca's bedroom.

Blanca stumbled, but quickly caught herself, grabbing what she needed and stuffing it in a satchel. "Be safe, Lyra. You know how he can be." She kissed her warmly on the cheek, embracing a few more precious seconds. Lyra was the closest thing she had to true family. It crushed Blanca to leave her.

But the thought of her father taking his anger out on Rose—as he had on Blanca and Lyra—steeled her resolve. She would protect her from that pain.

"Goodbye, darling." Lyra held her close before releasing her to snuggle her baby one last time. "Goodbye, my Rosebud." She kissed the baby's plump, dark cheek before returning her to Blanca's arms. "Be safe, and remember, I love you both dearly."

Blanca brushed away tears and escaped through the back door before she lost her courage. The air was cold, forcing a gasp from Blanca's freezing lungs. Making sure Rose was bundled well, Blanca took off into the forest, never once looking back.

"Rose!" Blanca shot upright, the word releasing a stream of poison from her mouth. How could she have forgotten about Rose? For a moment she was still running through the forest, clutching the baby to her chest, hoping to make it to the next village over. But the soft smoothness of the mattress beneath her said differently; she was still in the mage's home, or wherever he was keeping her. Taking a deep breath, she allowed the frigidness of the forest and the thundering of her heart to die away in the background.

"Another memory?" Randune rose from the corner where he had been observing. It seemed that was all he did, and Blanca found it disconcerting. As soon as she was able, she'd leave this place. "I did predict they'd be coming back in the next few days. An especially painful one, yes?" He walked over to her and readjusted the bubble which had gone askew after her flashback.

Blanca ignored his concern. "When you found me, was there anyone else? I remember a baby. One by the name of Rose. Deep brown skin, round and rosy cheeks, and a dimpled grin. She was my sister. I need to find her."

The man stroked his beard in thought. "An infant? We found you alone, collapsed in the snow. All that was beside you was a bitten-into apple. A vibrant scarlet one, actually. Rather beautiful." As if realizing he was rambling on, he hastily added, "I'm sorry."

Blanca sank back down, trying to force a memory to the front of her mind. Why had there been an apple? Where was Rose now? What happened to Lyra? Fear suddenly washed over her, bathing her in goosebumps. She had confessed pretty much everything to Randune. What if he told the king, or worse, her father? What if she was forced to return? The wisps of poison caught her attention. With this new power, her father could no longer harm her. A smile spread across her face.

He can't hurt me. The thought was almost too good to be true.

"Are you well, m'dear? I would not have thought the mention of the child possibly being missing would have made you smile." Randune furrowed his brows but eventually shrugged. "You're healing rapidly and should be able to leave your bed soon. I recommend another full day of bed rest, but my fellow mages beg to differ." His voice hinted annoyance, but she paid it no mind; it was the first time Blanca had heard him mention others.

"There are other mages here?" Blanca had heard of mages and the extraordinary gifts and abilities they possessed but had never seen one other than Randune. "So you worked together to bring me back to life?" Blanca still didn't quite believe that she had died and been brought back to life, but it was what Randune believed had happened, and he was a mage...

"Yes, there is myself and six others. They tend to be more reserved, and so let me do the explaining." Randune smiled. "And yes, they helped bring you back. It was more complicated than you might have realized. Tampering with death is never simple." He quietly left the room.

Complicated. Blanca understood that. It seemed her entire life was complicated. If Lyra was her stepmother, then that meant her real mother was dead. Her chest tightened at the thought. Even though she didn't remember her, it was like losing someone all over again. Had they been close? Had she known her at all? What memories had they shared? She wished that she could remember her mother instead of her father.

Her fingers gently traced the scars on her arms. She didn't remember how she had gotten all of them, but she knew who they were from. And there was still pain. Too much of it.

But she couldn't focus on the pain. She needed to find Rose as soon as possible. Randune had said she'd be ready to start walking around soon, so she could begin searching. And now she had the mages to help her find Rose. They had magic, so they must be able to.

Magic. What a terrifying concept. Was her poison breath magic? Blanca hadn't considered that. If it was, then she was breaking the law. That memory was quite clear:

Magic was not welcome.

The king would be furious with her. She didn't have permission to practice magic. Still, curiosity got the better of her. Removing the bubble around her head, she exhaled slowly. A light stream of mist issued forth, only visible with consistent, heavy breathing.

Blanca grinned, awed at how she was still able to breathe normally. Was she immune to all poisons now? While it would be interesting to test the theory, Blanca had already died once and had no interest in dying once more.

She experimented, discovering that laughter was the most potent and breathing was the least.

Soon the room was swimming with the poison, everything in a hazy film of green.

A slight popping noise caused Blanca to turn in surprise. She hadn't expected Randune to return so soon. But it wasn't Randune. Instead, a strange man was standing there, his hair a brilliant red, but his face turning a sickly shade of green.

The poison.

Blanca was stunned, too surprised by his abrupt entrance to help. With another popping sound, he appeared right next to her, gripping her arm tightly.

The room shifted, turning into multi-colored space, everything shifting and distorting, setting Blanca's head to pounding.

Then it was gone. Blanca staggered a bit, her bare feet curling as they came in contact with cold cobblestone. A soft wind blew, lifting her thin gown and raising goosebumps on her skin. Her legs shook, and she quickly sat down, preferring to bear the cold than to smash her head on the stones.

Looking around, Blanca noted that she was now in a courtyard, the darkness of the sky indicating nightfall. But hadn't it been only noon at Randune's home?

"Blanca! I've been waiting for your arrival for quite some time now," a smooth, feminine voice echoed, and Blanca tried to find its source. "There's no need to be frightened. At least not yet." Haunting laughter followed. This time Blanca pinned the sound as coming from a shadowy figure to her right.

"Who are you?" Blanca asked shakily, poison spilling out from between her lips. Knowing that she still retained this ability was some comfort, especially since she had no idea who she was talking to or where she was.

"Me? That's not important." The overcast skies allowed very little light, so Blanca inched forward, making out the frame of a chained woman. She was gaunt, bones visible even in the poor light. Her hair was a long tangled mess, reaching to the cobblestone.

"Who are you? Why am I here? I must get back." She preferred what she knew, and she didn't know much of anything right now.

The woman eyed her coldly. "You'll know everything soon enough. Just wait."

8

AURA

"AURA, I'M HUNGRY. We haven't eaten anything since our meat pies. And we've slept two times since then."

Aura inspected Aela's frail frame, noting that her face was unusually pale even for the under-fed little girl.

She had wanted to wait a while before venturing out again since the hooded ones would no doubt be searching for her. It was dangerous to use her gift on them, for magic was illegal in Allegora unless you were a mage and worked for the king.

"I promise I will go find something today, alright? We must be careful, though—Oobay is a dangerous place. If they were to find you, they would take you away from me. You understand that, don't you?"

Aerik and Aela nodded solemnly, their faces hollowed with hunger. Aura's heart bled at the sight; they were starving, all of them. She would have to take another risky venture to get food. They were definitely looking for her, so she would have to be extremely careful. Usually, it wasn't tough pick-pocketing a few coins here and there, but being a sixteen-year-old female was odd enough; she didn't need people wondering why she had ample funds.

"I'll take care of Aela while you're away, and she can take care of me." Aerik put an arm around the youngest and grinned. "We'll watch each other."

Aela frowned, her nose scrunching up. "Nope, I'll be in charge. And I'll make sure Aerik doesn't do anything crazy," she added, a smirk on her little features.

Aura grabbed them up into a big hug, her heart full of love for the little rascals. "You're both so brave. Mama and Papa would be proud. I promise I'll be back as soon as I can. Remember, if I don't return by the time the sun has come up again, go to Mam McPhobe's home. There should be a purse of coins under my bed. Take those with you and give them to her. She will keep you both safe until I return."

Aura knew there were no real coins in the purse; she would have used them for food already if there were. It was a coded message that Mam McPhobe would know meant that Aura's abilities had finally been discovered and that she was either dead or captured.

The woman owed Aura a favor for helping her fall asleep at night when she was unable to. Sleep was precious to the people of Oobay.

Falling asleep while working was deadly. Either the machinery or the hooded ones would kill you. It also meant punishment for your families. So, you got as much sleep as you possibly could and hoped that you wouldn't be the next one to die.

Aura had saved the favor for a day such as this. She had always worried her abilities would one day be found out and that she'd be hunted for them.

"Goodbye," she called as she exited their tiny home. "I'll be back soon." They shouted a cheerful response, bringing a smile to her face.

Jogging slowly to the end of the alley, Aura looked cautiously about, having seen firsthand where being hasty could get her.

The streets were busy, as usual, the heavy smog hanging like a floating blanket over the tops of the buildings. More people died from breathing in the noxious fumes that the factories constantly belched out than from the hooded ones. Still, the people still feared them more, for they had the power to send people to the palace, the one place that just might be worse than Oobay.

Everyone was going about their usual business, veils drawn across their faces to prevent the inevitable decay of their lungs. Everyone here worked in the factory unless they ran their own business, like the baker. Those who had their own occupation were extremely lucky and among the very few to have any real rights.

Freedom—it was something she craved. To be able to breathe deeply and never once catch a hint of burning wood or oiled metal.

"Hey, ye over there!" Aura turned to the grizzled older man pointing at her. "Whatcha doing standing there allowing ye mind ta wander! We've work to do, girl. There's nae time to dream." He shook his head sadly and hobbled on.

Aura scurried away, not wanting to cause a scene. Her mind went to the older man, her heart heavy. That man had probably never been allowed to dream. He had most likely worked in the factories his whole life, gotten married young, and had children who mostly died as infants. That was the grim reality of Oobay. Death would come, often in a horrific way. Dreaming was for those who wished to die.

Aura slid through the traffic of bodies, trying not to breathe in the smell of sweat and burnt clothing. Water was precious, so baths were rare. It was better to be hydrated than to be clean.

Once clear of the main stream of bodies, Aura wove through small streets, often running down alley short-cuts. The farther from the baker's street she was, she reasoned, the better chance she had of remaining undetected.

The delicious scent of roasting meat reached her first. Next followed the sweet smell of cooking onions. Aura's stomach rumbled, saliva pooling in her mouth. Only now did she realize just how hungry she was.

Allowing her nose to lead her, Aura came upon a small market, rusty metal carts lining the street. The city was dangerous this far north. No one with good intentions came this far unless this happened to be their home. But she'd come too far to leave now.

Taking a tentative step forward, Aura inspected the people who milled about the carts. For the most part, they appeared to be families with small children, their frames gaunter than her own. The children that stood sullenly about were far too young to be forced into factory work. There were some older men and women, their faces worn down in the customary hard lines and angles the factories gave to the people. Some carried shards of glass in their grip, as if afraid that at any moment they might be attacked. Considering where they were, the fear was valid.

There were too many nervous people around. Aura wouldn't be able to take food without being noticed. She could possibly force sleep on the entire street... She shook her head and laughed softly. A whole street? The most she had done was five people. Still, the image of Aela and Aerik being without food haunted her. They needed to eat, and soon. They were already weak enough as it was.

Aura took a deep breath and allowed herself to sense the consciousnesses of those on the street. Eleven altogether. Each pulsed with different emotions: anger, fear, sadness. The sheer diversity of emotions was overwhelming, but Aura didn't relinquish her hold. She focused her mind. Sleep, she commanded, allowing her own consciousness to roll over them. The people wavered, some falling asleep instantly—their weariness too hard to overcome—but others were more stubborn.

Sleep! she commanded again, forcing all her will upon them. There was a collective tumble. Opening her eyes, Aura saw that all had fallen to the ground. She had done it.

Her legs shook, and she fell down as well, the rock-strewn road biting into her knees, drawing blood. The breath knocked out of her, she lay there, energy gone.

The aroma of cooked meat wafted toward her, beckoning her to get up and keep moving. Stumbling up, she steadied herself against the rough brick wall of a building and made her way to one of the carts.

Her hands trembled as she opened it. Strips of hark lay in rows, steaming hot and tender to the touch.

Her limbs shook with gnawing, aching hunger. A wave of weariness passed over her, and she quickly grabbed onto the cart. She had to stay upright.

Unfolding a handkerchief, she laid five strips on it, moving on to the next cart. This one held potatoes. Baked with no seasoning, but Aura didn't mind. Three of these were added to the handkerchief.

She bit into the potato, ignoring how it burned her mouth. Besides, once she began eating, nothing could have stopped her. The potato was gone in a matter of moments, her mouth on fire.

Caution abandoned, Aura scampered over to the last cart, her energy partially restored. Her jaw dropped. Inside was a whole chakra, steamed to perfection. One bite was said to fill a man for hours. It was exactly what Aura needed. Using a knife to cut the large plant in half, she placed one on the overflowing handkerchief.

But wait, why was a chakra in this part of Oobay? No one from these parts could come close to being able to afford one.

"I suggest you put the knife down," a calm voice stated from behind her. Aura dropped the food and turned, knife still very much in her hand. A man stood in front of her. He was short, dressed in a simple green jerkin. What was most startling about his features was the brilliant red hair that looked like the last moment of a sunset before it disappeared. He was also oddly healthy, muscles evident in his arms and legs. Whoever he was, he was not from Oobay.

Aura reached out with her mind, prepared to lure him into slumber as well. When she probed his mind, however, she found his emotions frozen. She could not read them.

Pushing past the thought, Aura commanded him to sleep. She felt him waver, but he did not fall. His body would not accept sleep. Summoning all her strength again, Aura found that she was too hungry, too exhausted to force him. Her energy was gone, the one potato having gotten her as far as it could.

The man smiled and reached for her arm, Aura's half-stumble away a poor attempt at escape. In one moment, the city of Oobay disappeared in a hazy blur.

Suddenly, it was dark and cold. Aura wrapped her arms around herself in an attempt to warm up. Glancing around, everything was shadowy, wisps of fog skittering about. Where had he taken her?

Aela and Aerik. Her heart tore itself apart at the thought of them being harmed.

"No!" she screamed. "Bring me back! I have to go back!" She ran through a courtyard, her boots echoing on the stone floor. "Bring me back!" The panic lent strength to her limbs, adrenaline threatening to spill out of her veins.

"Hello to you too, my dear Aura." The voice stopped Aura in her tracks. "Yes, I do know your name. No, I will not tell you how I know.

You're the very last of my guests to arrive; did you know that? I've seen what you can do, and I must say, I'm quite impressed!"

Aura stepped closer to the voice, noting that it was coming from an older woman. She was chained to two pillars, gown in tatters, her hair a long, mangled mess. Her eyes were hauntingly beautiful, though, a deep, poisonous red like blood.

"I don't care! Just tell me where I am." Aura licked her lips and took a calming breath. She was growing more terrified by the minute, her limbs trembling from more than just exhaustion.

"Where?" The woman laughed again, the sound causing shivers to course down her spine. The woman's eyes danced with a crazed light, and her face was deathly pale. "Why, my dear girl, I would have thought you'd have figured it out. You're in Denthlire, the land of fog and smoke."

9

CERISE

CERISE AWOKE WITH a splitting headache. Rising from the hard floor, she winced, hand clasped to her head.

Hand. She was human again. Well, that was relieving. But where was she? Her vision swam as she tried to inspect her surroundings.

The floor was simple grey stone, freezing to the touch. The walls were the same stone but had intricate designs engraved into them. Upon closer inspection, it became obvious they clearly were carvings of war. Mankind and all manner of magical beings were locked in an epic battle, the details so exquisite, Cerise could almost hear their hoarse battle cries. On the ceiling above her was a beautiful mural of some sort of celebration. Beings of all shapes and sizes were frozen in dance, joy evident on their faces.

"I'm relieved to see you've awakened." The voice thundered in the stillness of the room, making Cerise flinch. Raised voices never meant anything good. She had to fight the urge to cower. *Raina's dead... Raina's dead... Raina's dead...*

But she knew that voice, and his scent... Cerise whirled—her fear replaced with rage—a growl rumbling deep within her chest. It was him. The one who took her.

"Easy there, little wolf." The red-headed man chuckled, his frame tense despite the easy expression on his face. "I am here on the orders of Madame Rose. She requests your presence. Should you refuse, I am to enforce by any means necessary." A cold smile appeared on his face.

Cerise stiffened, distrustful of the charismatic man. But now was not the time to start a scene, especially since she had absolutely no idea what was going on. "Very well, I will go with you. But know that I will rip your head off should I be given the slightest reason to." She glared as she strode out of the room and glanced about the large hall, the walls made of the same grey stone. They must be in a castle.

The man grinned and shut the door behind them. "I'm sure you will, little wolf."

Cerise realized soon enough that she wasn't alone. The courtyard was shrouded in fog, cool breezes causing shivers to ripple along her skin as she inspected her surroundings. There were three others with her, all females of various ages.

The one closest to her right was tall and at least twenty. Cerise couldn't help but gawk slightly at the toned muscles of her exposed arms. With her short brown hair and cold grey eyes, she was unlike any of the other young women Cerise had ever seen in her village. She reminded her of the leaves before a storm, a warning to flee before danger struck.

Immediately to her left was a shorter young woman, but then again, all of them appeared short compared to the first one, who had to have been at least six feet.

This girl had waist-long black hair that rippled slightly in the breeze. Her skin was a deep, rich brown, and her large eyes matched it. If one were to go just on looks, she was absolutely stunning, but she must have been terrified as she had yet to stop trembling.

The last girl was perhaps the most curious. Her eyes kept shifting about, clearly alert to everything going on. She was the shortest of all, with shoulder-length black hair and beautiful almond-shaped brown eyes. Her frame was so slight, it was difficult at first to tell if she was female. Bones protruded against the crude fabric of her dress, and her face was gaunt. Pity filled Cerise. No one should have to live how this girl must have had to.

"Why are we here?" demanded the tall one, her voice managing to be intimidating and nonchalant at once. "Who do you work for?"

Cerise realized she was addressing the man, who had slipped in behind them. He smirked. "Why don't I let her introduce herself." Cerise frowned in confusion. *The courtyard was empty.*

"Hello, m'dears. I'm delighted you all could make it here today. I am Madame Rose." The smooth, yet haunting, voice echoed from a shrouded corner of the courtyard. Upon closer inspection, Cerise made out the emaciated form of a woman.

Cerise stepped forward slightly, examining the woman. At one point, she must have been exquisitely beautiful, with long dark hair, full red lips, and a figure that—though now wasted—must have at one point been quite enviable.

"I have hired you for this grand scheme. I apologize for the forceful abductions, but you see, it was necessary we spirit you away with as little excitement as possible. Though I must say, each of you gave Pan quite a deal of trouble." She chuckled softly as she glanced at the man who stood resolutely behind them all.

Pan. So that was the man's name. Cerise made a point to glare once more at him, but he just smiled in return. Fury boiled up inside her. What she wouldn't give to rip that smirk right off his face.

"You spoke of a scheme," the pretty, long-haired girl said, wisps of green escaping from between her lips. Cerise's brows furrowed in confusion. Was it magic? If she had abilities, and so did Cerise... did they all? The thought was disconcerting. Magic wasn't exactly welcomed in Allegora.

"Yes, I did indeed speak of a scheme. As you may or may not be able to see, I am chained to these pillars. There is an item that can free me from these shackles, and you shall get it for me."

"Really? There's only one thing that can free you?" Cerise snorted in disbelief. The woman who had a teleporting bodyguard to do her bidding couldn't free herself from some chains?

Madame Rose leveled her gaze at her, a shudder running unbidden down Cerise's spine.

"Well, the Saber of Ihotem would work as well, but its last known location was the bottom of the Evanscenian Sea." Her voice rose to a screech, eyes glinting red. "Or perhaps you'd like to find the Staff of Careine. It shouldn't be too hard, as long as you're willing to decipher all five hundred and thirty-six clues left scattered around Atulau and written in a forgotten language."

An awkward silence fell over them as Madame Rose finished and dread sunk low in Cerise's gut as she realized how unprepared she was.

"Thank you for that enlightening explanation," the tall one responded sarcastically. "Now why in Denthlire are we here?"

A laugh sounded from behind them, and Cerise turned to see Pan. "My apologies," he said, grinning. "You have no idea how ironic that is."

Everything fell into place and a chill swept through her body.

They were in Denthlire.

Cerise took a long, shuddering breath, focusing all her willpower on not panicking. Deep breath in, deep breath out. Everything was going to be okay; all she had to do was focus on what was going on around her. Still, the name itself made dread build up in her stomach—a tumultuous sea that threatened to make its way out of her mouth.

"You say we must retrieve this item for you, but why can't your precious bodyguard?" the grey-eyed one asked again, and Cerise had to admire her boldness. "I have seen his teleporting abilities; it should be simple enough." The woman frowned, and Cerise began to wonder if that was all the expression she showed.

"And what makes you think we'll help you?" Cerise added. "For all we know, you could be a criminal that the king has imprisoned here."

Madame Rose smiled, but it was forced, her eyes glittering coldly. "Unfortunately, I cannot command Pan to retrieve it for me. You can thank your mages for that. Since they were unable to kill me or Pan, making sure neither of us had the power to free me was the worst thing they could—"

"Why now, though?" the tall one interrupted. "It makes no sense."

Madame Rose glowered darkly before continuing. "It was the worst punishment they could inflict." Her gaze fell on Cerise, the crazed delight of it making her wish to shrink back.

"Pan, these girls are the fourth group, correct? Or maybe the fifth… things do get muddled after a couple hundred years or so." She turned to him, locking eyes with him until he nodded in agreement. "The others… didn't succeed. Actually, most of them didn't survive the first day. But that was when we were still looking for the exact location. We know now, which should be helpful to you all."

They weren't the first ones? Cerise's stomach churned. How had she jumped from one terrible situation right into another?

"Absolutely not. Kill us for all I care, but I refuse to be the savior of the woman who kidnapped us." The tall one stepped forward, the venom in her voice sparking courage inside Cerise.

"Me too," she declared, fighting down her worry. "I'd rather die then help you." With two having stepped forward, the short one did as well, and finally the one with the long hair. Standing all together, Cerise felt her confidence surge, until she heard laughter.

It echoed through the courtyard, filling it with its shrill, skin-crawling sound. "What bravery," Madame Rose mocked. "Do you feel strong standing up to me? Does it make you feel unstoppable?

"Verre," Madame Rose turned to the grey-eyed one. "It would be a pity if Baen should die in a freak accident involving one of his inventions." The warrior paled, her eyes sparkling dangerously.

"Blanca," now she turned to the long-haired girl. "I know where Lyra and Rose are, though you may not. Aura, your siblings miss you."

The short girl, Aura, lunged for Madame Rose but was caught by Pan. "I swear if you—"

Madame Rose simply rolled her eyes and let her gaze fall once more on Cerise. "Cerise, darling. How is your mother these days?"

Fear washed over Cerise, but anger soon took control. How did this woman know so much about them? So much about her?

"Don't you dare touch her! You vile, despicable monster!" Cerise growled, feeling fur grow on her body, her ears perking up and reshaping. A restraining arm clasped her shoulder, a warning not to try anything. Pan, who had somehow managed to sneak up on her. Again.

Swallowing hard, Cerise squeezed her eyes shut, a violent shudder running through her body as she commanded herself to remain calm.

Madame Rose was right—Pan could kill her mother in the blink of an eye should she say or do one wrong thing. She already stood in perilous waters without killing the woman.

Eyes snapping open, she was welcomed by shocked and even terrified stares. Nervousness gnawed at her stomach when the looks didn't disappear. Running a hand subconsciously over her head, it dawned on her—wolf ears were not normal.

"Is everyone calm now?" Madame Rose's tranquil voice was nearly enough to cause Cerise to lose control completely, but she couldn't afford that. Her mother's life was too precious. "I'd hate to have to kill everyone so soon."

Blanca and Aura tried vainly to keep their expressions neutral, but Cerise was glad to know she wasn't the only one who was enraged. Verre... she was someone Cerise could not quite figure out. It was like she was made of cherry wood, strong and unyielding. Cerise could not tell what fazed her and what didn't. And though she had no idea what it was they were stealing, she was glad to have her on her side.

"Madame Rose." The deep, raspy voice of Aura was a bit shocking, especially since it came from such a small frame. "What exactly is it that we are stealing for you?"

Madame Rose chuckled. "I'm so glad you asked! What I need is a pair of very red, very powerful shoes. Dorthea's slippers to be precise." She spat out the name, not hiding her hatred of it.

Cerise was surprised. What could Madame Rose possibly hate about the greatest mage of all time?

10

VERRE

DORTHEA'S RED SLIPPERS? The insane old woman had to be joking. Regrettably, insane people had a tendency to be dangerous, and Verre preferred to deal with those that could be dispatched simply. It had crossed her mind to drive a glass shard through the woman's heart, but at the mention of Baen, her own heart had stopped.

If this woman knew about her husband, then who knew what she would do to her family, including her mother and father?

"What!" squeaked Blanca. "*The* Dorthea?"

Verre had to agree with Blanca's sentiment on this one. The slippers were one of the most famous items in the history of Allegora, as well as one of its most powerful magical weapons.

At least, that's what every legend stated. The slippers had been locked away in a hidden vault by the royal family centuries back. To try to steal them would be suicide. The other objects she had spoken of, like the Saber of Ihotem, Verre had only heard stories about, and even those were thought to just be exaggerated tales. The slippers, however, were well-known.

"Yes, Blanca, the slippers created by the mage Dorthea." Madame Rose smiled, though it was obviously forced, her skin stretching rather grossly over her wide jaw. "I need them in order to escape my prison. And remember, should you try to attack me, Pan is under orders to make himself... *familiar* with your families."

Verre grit her teeth, striving to remain calm and collected. "You've already made it quite clear that we have no choice but to carry out your wishes." The one called Cerise seemed to be having trouble containing her rage as well, as she gave only a clipped nod in agreement.

"Good. I like to think that this doesn't have to end in death." Madame Rose's voice caught slightly on the last word, and for a second, Verre was able to glimpse decades of anguish. A slight shudder ran down her spine. What had the mages done to this woman?

Almost immediately, though, the look was extinguished, replaced with a trained, neutral one that Verre was all too familiar with herself. "Training will commence immediately—I will only allow you to leave when I find you at least somewhat competent—and then it's off to Allegora to steal my beloved slippers!"

Off to Allegora… The words reminded her of an important fact: they were in Denthlire. Something twisted sharply inside of Verre, and she realized that it was fear. Hearing about the famed land of fog and smoke was one thing, but being there was another. Home had never sounded so inviting. "Your rambling is wasting precious time that we could be using to train and prepare." Verre shifted her stance slightly, locking eyes with Madame Rose.

"What an intelligent person you are." Madame Rose smiled, though her eyes hardened at Verre's snarky tone. "I am pleased I chose you for this mission, or heist, as I fondly call it. I've had my eye on you since you were but a small child. Glass. What a fitting gift for one so cold that she might shatter at any moment."

The woman was an absolute lunatic. There was no doubt about it. Still, a slight shudder ran through Verre at the mention of being frail. She had trained, fought, and sacrificed so much to be *strong*. One simple phrase from a complete stranger wouldn't change that.

"When do we begin training?" Cerise asked, her tone wary. Verre had to respect the guts of the young woman, standing up to Pan and his frightening abilities. Even Aura had spoken up. But Blanca… Verre glanced at her. She seemed like the kind of girl who wasn't used to hard work. She had hardly spoken a word since they had entered, and she was now standing quietly, her face a perfect picture of fear. Verre could only hope she survived. She herself had every intention of getting back to Baen and her parents, preferably in one piece.

"Training begins now. This castle has been abandoned for over a thousand years, so there's plenty of space for you all. Food around here is decidedly lacking, but Pan makes daily jumps to Allegora to collect some. You may think I'm a cold-blooded monster, but those slippers are extremely important to me, so I'm willing to risk everything to retrieve them. You all must know that feeling to a certain extent, that desire." Her eyes glinted as she spoke, showcasing their red tinge, like blood newly spilled from an open wound.

"You are most certainly a monster." The sweet voice of Blanca caught Verre off-guard, especially with the rage that saturated her tone. "You have threatened to kill men, women, and young children in a matter of moments. No one, no thing, other than a monster, would ever say that." Green mist seeped from between her lips, permeating the air.

Verre took a cautious step back, wary of what the mist contained. Surprisingly, Pan did not engage Blanca. Instead, he hung back, his eyes fastened on the mist. Was that fear she saw flash in his eyes? What was it about Blanca that made him so cautious? According to what she had seen, his body could heal rapidly.

Madame Rose sighed. "Must we stoop so low as to insult one another? I am offering you a chance to see your loved ones again, simple as that. Speak out of turn once more, and precious baby Rose—how sweet of you to name her after me—will be no more. Now, please, stop talking. None of us wish to inhale poison."

Poison. Verre took another calculated step away from Blanca. So that was what poured out of her mouth. It seemed Pan was also vulnerable to it. Verre tucked that information away; it could prove useful.

So, now she knew of Cerise's and Blanca's abilities; shape-shifter and poison spewer. All she needed to figure out was Aura's. She was a strange girl, her eyes never settling in one place. Someone who didn't trust. Very much like herself, but did that make Aura a threat? Verre would find out soon enough, but in the meantime, she'd be cautious.

"May we proceed to training now? This conversation is tedious," Cerise stated, crossing her arms. Verre wondered if she permanently frowned, or if it just seemed that way. The young woman was short, taller only than Aura. Her smooth brown skin held a scattering of large freckles, her round face framed by short and frizzy curls. There was a fierce beauty about her, like something that belonged somewhere wide open and airy, where she could run until her legs gave out.

"Yes, training. My, my, you're an energetic bunch." Madame Rose chuckled, the sound becoming increasingly revolting the more it happened. "Pan, escort them to the ballroom; I believe that shall suffice."

He gave a curt nod and began guiding the girls out of the courtyard. Cerise tensed, a low growl vibrating low in her throat. Everyone stiffened, the tension thick in the air. But as if remembering what Madame Rose had promised to do, she stopped, her shoulders slumped.

Verre refused to walk in front of Pan, quite willing to believe he'd stab her in the back—literally—if he had the chance.

As they walked, Verre got a closer look at the castle. The stone throughout the entire building was unusual. When Verre studied it closely, it seemed to emit a soft glow. Perhaps it was a natural mineral found only in Denthlire.

There was also a constant shriek that filled the air, keeping Verre's nerves on edge. Perhaps it was simply the wind, but given where they were, it was best to remain on guard. Who knew what sort of monsters lurked in dark corners.

Verre had been in many strange places in her line of work, but Denthlire won as the strangest, though perhaps not the most frightening.

She had only ever heard stories of the mythical place, how being sent there made one go mad, bringing on hallucinations of the strongest sort. Looking back, it appeared Madame Rose might have been suffering from them herself.

"There are a few rules that must be obeyed," Pan said quietly as they entered a cavernous room. At one point, it must have been absolutely stunning, but due to time and neglect, the gold of the molding was chipped and the vibrant hues that had danced about the walls were muted, like ghosts of a glorious past.

"One: Madame Rose is the final authority on everything, and I will be sure to enforce anything she commands. Two: you are to respect me as your trainer. If I say you're wrong, you're wrong. You'll only have one shot at this, and it is necessary that it works. Three: Denthlire is dangerous. Only this castle remains safe. Should you decide to venture out into the rest of this land, even I won't attempt to find you."

So Denthlire was as deadly as everyone had assumed. Verre had no intention of leaving the castle. Yet. First, she would need to plan and prepare. There had to be another way to escape this land of fog and smoke, and she would have to find it. Baen was probably worried sick, hoping that she had just left for another job and had forgotten to say goodbye. She could see his dark eyes now, so sorrowful. As much as she hated to admit it, this whole ordeal was terrifying. No one had ever bested her, much less kidnapped her. But everything was going to be perfectly fine. All she had to do was remain calm.

"Shall we begin then?" Verre stepped forward, glancing back at the other young women. They all looked up at her, rather nervously in fact. Cerise would do fine, and so would Aura; they were both survivors. And Blanca… Verre smiled at the fog that puffed out with her nervous breathing. She just might end up being their greatest weapon.

11

BLANCA

BLANCA WAS UTTERLY terrified. First, she had been swept away to a strange land, only to discover it was quite possibly the most secluded and terrifying place she had ever been to.

Second, she was now being forced to steal one of the most powerful magical objects to exist; if she refused, her family would be brutally slain.

But, she doubted this was the most frightening experience she had ever had. Even with her fragmented memory, there were scars on her shoulders and arms that couldn't have a happy story behind them.

Blanca looked around the ballroom. The one woman, Verre, seemed quite at ease, executing a few warm-ups with strength and elegance. Blanca had always prided herself on her excellent figure, but it seemed an excellent figure alone wasn't going to get her anywhere when it came to training. She couldn't even practice with her abilities, considering the deadly potency of them.

"Blanca," the wolf-girl called. "Perhaps we can spar together?"

Swallowing nervously, Blanca nodded. Ever since the wolf-girl had shifted, Blanca had been wary. She didn't know why, but shape-shifters unsettled her. Just seeing someone morph into something else made her heart freeze with fear. Maybe she'd remember why at some point, but she wasn't entirely certain she even wanted to.

Of the four of them who had been captured, Verre and the wolf-girl seemed the most adept, as if they had done this violent sort of thing before. If she was to practice, she would have preferred Aura, who at least seemed slightly nervous herself. At least it wasn't Verre, though, who at that moment was summoning glass shards and throwing them expertly into the wall ahead of her.

"I'm Cerise, in case you didn't remember. Judging from your face, I'm guessing fighting isn't something you're accustomed to?" The curly-haired girl smiled softly, though even Blanca could tell it was forced; all lips, no eyes. She couldn't blame her, though. They all were in a strange and new environment. No one knew who to trust, especially Blanca. They were all too confident, too deadly.

Shaking her head slowly, Blanca gestured to her throat. The slight paling of Cerise's features was enough for Blanca to understand that she knew of the deadliness of her breath. This quest, or "heist," as the strange Madame Rose called it, was going to be difficult if she could not converse with the others.

"How about we start with some simple warm-ups to get the blood flowing? I'll be certain to go slowly so that you can learn. We're going to need all the help we can get if we're to survive this." Cerise chuckled softly and shrugged.

The speech was such an exceedingly common one that Blanca grinned. It seemed motivational speeches were not Cerise's strong suit; however, any form of public speaking had been Blanca's. Though the days she had been able to speak without fear of being hit—or even now, afraid of killing someone—were like a pleasant dream that was achingly just beyond reach.

Readying herself for the spar, Blanca followed the simple warm-up steps Cerise provided. Stretching arms, bending legs, inhaling, exhaling. Blanca had to remain cautious and not breathe too hard. Normal breathing usually wasn't toxic enough to harm, but she didn't want to take any chances, not with Lyra and Rose's lives on the line. As it was, her dress was a nuisance, getting in the way of the physical exercise. She was beginning to understand why the rest all wore trousers.

Cerise balled her hands into fists, the kind expression on her face turning cold. "Ready?"

Blanca gulped, breaking out in a sweat. She was not a warrior; fighting was not her style, not at all. But she needed to make sure Lyra and Rose would remain safe. Nodding slowly, Blanca tensed, clenching her own hands into fists.

Cerise struck out without warning, Blanca barely ducking under the lightning-fast punch. Thoroughly scared, Blanca backed away from Cerise. This wasn't how she expected training to go. Cerise came at her again, this time the solid blow finding its way towards Blanca's soft abdomen. With a groan she keeled over, hand clutched to her stomach. Poison spilled from between her lips, causing Cerise to step back in fright. Glad for the momentary respite, Blanca choked, the wind knocked out of her. This only made the poison worse, but she couldn't help it; her body needed more oxygen.

"Stop!" Cerise commanded sharply, still moving back carefully. "That's not fair. You don't see me turning into a wolf, do you?"

Blanca shook her head vigorously. It wasn't her fault that merely breathing could harm others. She hadn't asked for such a curse. And it was a curse, not some gift like Madame Rose liked to think. No, it was a horrid curse. "Please don't—I can't control it." The words were spoken in a whisper, but poison still poured out.

Cerise's hard expression softened, sympathy in her eyes. "I know what it's like to not be able to control something. Usually I don't even remember what happened."

Blanca's eyes widened. Cerise, one of the ones who seemed so confident, actually had trouble with control? She smiled hesitantly, unsure of how to respond, if she should respond at all. She decided on simply nodding her head, a gesture Cerise seemed to understand the meaning behind.

"Want to try that again? You're fast, you just need to remain focused. If I was able to survive alone in the forest of Lithrium, you can learn to dodge a blow." Cerise returned to her initial stance, her face the same hard look, except now Blanca could detect a glimmer of a smile as well.

Blanca did not wish to try again—she didn't even want to be here. But for now, she was stuck in Denthlire, and she most certainly wasn't going to be able to find a way to escape if she couldn't even block a punch from Cerise. Rising from the ground, Blanca nodded, a grimace on her face.

Cerise struck again, her blows blindingly fast.

Blanca ducked, but this time she didn't drop her guard. Cerise was fierce and quick, and she didn't relish the thought of another bruise on her stomach. Cerise aimed a kick at Blanca's waist, which was again dodged. Feeling slightly more confident, Blanca began to assess any weak points she could exploit. Even thinking such a thought sent a thrill racing down Blanca's spine; this was something out of a book!

"Your form is pathetic," Cerise remarked, drawing away. "If you're going to throw a punch, don't close your fist over your thumb, unless you want to break it."

Heat rose up Blanca's neck as she readjusted. "Like this?"

"Not even close." Cerise grabbed her hands and wrapped her fingers into fists. "Here you go. Remember, don't put all your strength into the first blow. Use it to assess, and then come at them with your other fist. Also, don't go for the face."

Clench fists, no thumbs, not face. This was way too confusing. Still, after a readying gulp of air, she swung for Cerise's abdomen.

"Not bad," commented Cerise as she threw another punch, this one clipping Blanca's ribs. "With time, you could be quite proficient."

Trying to ignore the warm, happy feeling the compliment gave her, Blanca focused on dodging kicks and blows, and it was far more difficult than she could have imagined. After but a few minutes, Blanca was sore, knowing bruises would appear soon enough.

"Ready to take a break?" Cerise was breathing evenly, though a shine of sweat could be seen on her brow. "I could use some water."

She wiped her face with the back of her hand, and Blanca noticed that Cerise's blouse was soaked in sweat; hers was too.

Pan appeared to their right, wisps of grey shadows the only reminder of the magic he had used. "There is a jug of water by the left wall of the ballroom. Feel free to partake as you wish. From what I've observed, you need work, but with time you could excel." He glanced over the young women with a half-smile. For some reason, his smiles were always dark, as if he knew a deadly secret that no one else did.

Verre snorted, throwing a spiraling glass shard directly into a makeshift target. Another perfect throw. "I doubt I need any extra training. I've been doing this—the missions, or as you call them, heists—for quite some time, so please, don't insult my skill with your mediocre analysis."

Eyes wide, Blanca gaped at Verre. Didn't she know how powerful he was? Pan strode slowly over to Verre, his eyes scanning her, analyzing her. Blanca thought he would say something, perhaps challenge Verre to a duel, but, as if satisfied with what he saw, he simply smiled and walked away.

"You."

Blanca panicked as she realized that Verre was calling her. Thinking it best to comply, Blanca hurried over, a thousand scenarios racing through her head.

"Your ability is poison, yes?"

Confused, Blanca nodded, unsure as to why Verre was smiling. The warrior woman's smile was frightening indeed, almost more so than Pan's. However, she knew very little about either, a fact that was equally terrifying.

"That's good. Just keep training, understood? I might be able to teach you some things myself." Verre smiled as if she thought that would reassure her, but all it did was frighten Blanca more. The woman was intimidating, and it wasn't just her height. There was a commanding air about her, a deadly silence.

Blanca didn't know how to react. Verre's tone sent a shiver coursing down her spine. Nothing about this place felt right.

AURA

AURA HAD SEEN many strange things in her life, but being stuck in Denthlire with other magical humans—while being trained to steal a magical pair of slippers—was something she never expected to see herself doing. At all.

She took a swig from one of the smaller flasks Pan had provided, allowing herself to relish the sweet coolness of water. People had said Denthlire was quite literally a nightmare, but Aura found it to be remarkably pleasant compared to Oobay.

Placing the flask on the smooth floor, Aura noticed Verre's penetrating stare. The woman intimidated her, and Aura had gone toe-to-toe with some of the most vile slave traders and hooded ones. The woman was tall and pure muscle, qualities Aura was sorely lacking, though she often tried to deny her frailty. Verre motioned her over, worry knotting in Aura's stomach.

"You. You're Aura, correct? I have seen everyone else's abilities. What exactly can you do?" Verre flicked her fingers, a small glass crystal forming in the palm of her hand. It was beautiful and perfectly shaped, glittering coldly in the soft light.

No nonsense or meaningless talk. Verre was all business, something that seemed obvious now that Aura thought about it.

"Mine is glass if that wasn't obvious already. I find it to be the perfect weapon." Verre smiled, causing a slight shudder to run down Aura's back.

What was the reason for asking her? Verre didn't seem the type to just chat away. No, she had an ulterior motive, one that was no doubt beneficial only to herself. It was a negative assumption, and she had only known Verre for an extremely short amount of time, but Aura had never been able to afford to think positively. That was true now more than ever. But perhaps it could be beneficial to gain an ally and show her strength. Verre seemed like the kind of person to value that.

"I can reach into the minds of others and force sleep upon them. It's a handy gift, especially for stealing." There was a small flicker of interest evident in Verre's grey eyes, but it disappeared almost instantly.

"Fascinating. Does it work for everyone? Can a person fight against your command of sleep?"

Verre's intrigue was confusing, especially since Aura had never really considered that. Was it possible for someone to rebel against sleep? Pan had managed to, but only for a short time. If he hadn't teleported so quickly, she most likely could have forced him into sleep. Looking around, Aura realized she could command them all to sleep with just a thought should she want to. The idea was both exhilarating and frightening.

"Someone can resist for a time, but eventually they will succumb." Aura allowed a half-smirk to creep across her features. If living in Oobay had taught her anything, it was to prove that you were needed, and to fight with everything in you to make sure that it wasn't stolen from you. Verre was terrifying, but Aura was determined to show her that she was necessary.

Verre watched her silently for a moment before nodding. "You will suffice. Now, you seem intelligent and agile, but we need to shape those raw elements into something more... something better. Do you trust me?"

Aura considered for a moment. Verre was extremely skilled, and Aura could use some training, considering that there was a great chance that they could all be brutally slain during this heist. "I trust your skill, but I don't trust you."

Verre chuckled, spinning a glass shard expertly. "Smart."

<hr>

The banquet table was practically groaning under the weight of the food, but Aura was too sore, too exhausted to even enjoy the pleasing aroma. She had expected Verre to be a tough trainer, helping her to achieve her true potential, but she had not expected her to be a cruel monster who worked her to the bone for two hours straight.

The clatter of utensils as Blanca and Cerise seated themselves helped her refocus, and the delicious smell of food began to revive her senses. Her weary eyes took in the brilliant display. Steaming hark glistening in golden sauce, blood-red berries' with leathery skins that were almost bursting, and all manner of vegetables cooked in various ways lay across the table.

Starving, Aura hurried to her seat at the long ironwood table, noting that Verre had done likewise.

She carved a large portion of hark onto a simple wooden plate—in stark contrast to the faded grandeur of the dining hall—and heaped a generous serving of crescent berries onto her plate as well, one tumbling to the ground. There was only water in the chipped glass jugs, but Aura's eyes lit up when she tasted it. It was fresh water, lacking the dusty taste that had saturated everything in Oobay. The food was so vibrant, Aura had a difficult time believing it was real. She had only ever seen colors this vivacious when wandering by a lord's front window.

When she shoved a piece of hark into her mouth, her taste buds nearly exploded in ecstasy. The meat was soft, melting in her mouth, leaving behind subtle hints of citrus and the savory taste of garlic. Aura sighed with pure delight before taking another bite, her fingers already ripping open the skin of a crescent berry. Red juice oozed out, staining her fingers. She quickly spooned the tender flesh of the fruit and popped it into her mouth. Her eyes widened at the tangy freshness. It was like consuming a warm spring day, complete with the sunshine and gentle breeze. Not that she really knew what that felt like, though she had fantasized about it often enough.

Looking up from her food, she caught a curious glance from Blanca. Judging from the way she carried herself, and the fact that she was using the utensils—her fingers poised elegantly—Aura guessed she was a noble.

The thought soured her stomach. Nobles received everything: money, power, food, and clothing. The king blessed them with an abundance of things, more than they possibly had a use for. And never once did they help those beneath them, those who worked in the mines, factories, palace. Instead, they ignored them, turning a blind eye to the pain and poverty the common people were subject to.

Swallowing another bite of hark, Aura refused to let such a thought ruin this meal. Blanca looked away with a blush—perhaps feeling ashamed for staring—and continued to eat.

Aura glanced over the table, spotting some bluras. Its pale blue color contrasted the rich orange pool of melted butter. Eyes wide in delight, she reached over and grabbed the bowl heaped with the mashed vegetable.

Spooning a portion onto her empty plate, she inhaled deeply and smelled the delicious earthiness of it, tinged with the scent of garlic. She used her fingers as a spoon and scooped some into her mouth. It was warm and soft, bringing contentment to Aura's already bursting stomach. For a moment, Aura forgot about the ache in her muscles, the ominous mission, and getting back to her siblings. Right now she was safe, full, and happy.

"Be careful," Cerise commented, bringing a forkful of hark to her own mouth. "If you eat too much, you'll likely vomit it up later."

Aura wanted to disagree, but what Cerise had said was true. Already her stomach churned, unused to quality food filling it. Sadly glancing down at the bluras, she pushed the plate away, not trusting her self-control.

If only Aerik and Aela could have been able to partake of the feast. Her heart clenched, hoping that they had listened to her and gone to Mam McPhobe's. She had no idea how long she would be stuck here. All appetite fled her as she imagined Aela crying herself to sleep, her little body shaking, or Aerik trying to be brave for his little sister, but also shedding tears, wondering if Aura would ever return.

She pushed away from the table, avoiding the curious stares that followed. The magnitude of everything that was going on was overwhelming, driving her heart and mind insane. If she didn't survive this, her siblings would die. Mam McPhobe was only supposed to be a temporary solution should she ever get captured. Once the woman found out that she wasn't coming back, she'd ship Aerik off to the factories and Aela... Aura hurried out of the dining hall, her eyes shut tightly against the thought. Aela would be sent to the palace.

Lost in the labyrinth of the cold and seemingly taunting halls, Aura continued to run, her muscles screaming for respite. Images rushed by, centuries past carved into the walls. Bloodshed, war, peace. A never-ending cycle, it seemed. Allegora had suffered from a civil war a millennia before, the magical beings against the humans. They had reached a compromise, the House of Rymere coming into power. At least, that's what her father had said. He had loved Allegorian history.

Aura slowed down, allowing her eyes to catch more of the stories and engravings. War. That was what Allegora was known for.

As she shoved open a large door, her stomach finally revolted and sent her crashing to the floor. Her knees bit into the cold stone as she vomited. Over and over she retched, her body trembling. After a few minutes of resting on the cool floor, she wiped her mouth and scanned her surroundings.

Everywhere there was darkness, but in wisps and shadows, constantly convulsing and twirling. It was cold. The kind of cold that struck deep into Aura's bones, leaving them aching. But what was most frightening were the shapes. Dark, whispering ghosts of beings, appearing for a moment, only to then blink out of existence.

The land was dead, stretching out in rolling plains of fog, making it impossible to truly see what the terrain was like. No plant, no light, no creatures—at least nothing physical. That was when Aura realized why Pan had not followed her.

There was no escape from this place.

13

CERISE

SLEEP DID NOT come easily in this place. There was no day or night, which frustrated Cerise. The wolf within her itched to be released so that she could explore, allowing her legs to run as fast as she could, as far away as she could get.

For once, Cerise was glad to have the wolf. Its fierce, predator-like side was actually comforting in this dangerous place. She got up from her bed, opening the door quietly as she slipped out.

All of them were antsy, hating how confining it was to be within the stone walls, but Cerise suffered the most, having only ever lived in a forest where she could roam as she pleased.

Apparently Madame Rose wanted personal progress reports, so Cerise had to meet with her as often as was deemed necessary. Even hearing her voice made Cerise wish to both snarl and flee. She was no ordinary human; that was the only fact Cerise was certain about.

Aura had staggered back inside the castle the night before, the girl's fear and resignation all that Cerise needed in order to know that Denthlire was all she had imagined. When she went to bed that night— her eyes fastened on the mural above her head—she could hear the mournful howls and piercing shrieks that seemed to echo through the empty and forlorn castle.

Whatever creatures prowled through Denthlire were no longer in Allegora for a reason. It was the dumping ground for all evil, and those that managed to survive the first day were not the sort of creatures Cerise had any intention of meeting.

Wandering through the halls, muscles tired from training, Cerise stopped to inspect the engravings. They were everywhere, invading each and every part of the lonely castle.

Some told stories from Allegora, stories Cerise's father used to tell her. Of the dragon who had betrayed her kind by warning the mages of a plan to destroy Allegora. Of the dwarf king who had set out to conquer Allegora, but was thwarted by the elf princess who had just inherited the throne. Of the Evanscenian seas that held mysteries that no creature knew. Cerise's favorite had always been the story of how the mages first began.

The memories made her heart twist within her, tears burning at the edges of her eyes so that she had to swipe them away hastily.

Before Allegora turned into a thriving country, it was constantly bathed in the blood of countless creatures. It was the battlefield for many a war.

One day, Lyol, a Seer dragon, flew over the land and noticed how the ground was red from so much carnage. Alighting, it took in the landscape and decided that it would make a beautiful kingdom. Then came the vision, a vision of all creatures, both magical and mundane, living in harmony.

The dragon evoked a spell that shook the universe, removing the blood from the land and forming the first humans. Lyol also created mages along with them. Both were children of war, born of the blood of many a battle.

These new and powerful beings were the first to turn the wasteland into a habitable place: Allegora. The Seer ordered that the mages protect Allegora, making it a safe haven for all. As news spread of the land inhabited by new and strange people, those from Evanscene and Moorehaven flocked to it, thus bringing about an age of peace.

Cerise trailed a hand along the engraving for the story, marveling at the size of Lyol. Dragons had long since disappeared from Allegora, though occasionally some drunk would claim to have seen one.

The Ancient Ones, the very first of the dragons, were said to live deep underground or so high up that their wings would graze the stars. Of course, no one knew for sure. They were only stories, and stories had a way of dressing up the truth.

"Studying the carvings? You are the first to do so in over a millennium. Besides me, of course."

Cerise whirled around, heart hammering in her chest. Pan stood there, hands crossed. He always appeared so silently. With how much resistance she had put up, Cerise didn't doubt that he had considered slitting her throat on more than one occasion. She definitely had thought the same of him.

Biting back a witty retort, she smiled. "Yes, they're quite beautiful. What I don't understand, though, is why they're here? And why is there a castle in the place that is simply for doing away with the evil in Allegora?" Cerise couldn't have been the only one who found a huge and elaborate castle in the middle of the land of fog and smoke strange. Everything about this place was mysterious, and it was driving her mad.

"Denthlire has a beautiful and rich history that few Allegorians know of. This place wasn't always the dumping ground for Allegora's waste. It was the pinnacle of magical knowledge; even the Ancient Ones would come to learn and to teach. It was a peaceful land, full of beauty and wisdom." His tone turned thoughtful, his expression almost wistful before turning dark.

"Then your people brought ruin upon it, their mages at the forefront. They thirsted for power and coveted our gifts, the gifts of healing and of intellect. They cursed the land so that it would never again bring forth life of any kind.

"Our queen fought back, desperate to hold onto her kingdom. There was a battle between her and Dorthea, the greatest mage of your people. Their battle fragmented the universe, separating Denthlire from Allegora, Moorehaven, Evanscene, and Ookramok," Pan stated quietly. His evident sorrow shocked Cerise.

Ookramok? It was real? She had always been told it was the supposed birthplace of all dragons. Moorehaven and Evanscene she knew about, though. They were the other two countries that helped make up Atulau.

"Was this your home?" She hadn't known that Denthlire had once been habitable, and she most certainly couldn't imagine it being a place of learning.

Pan turned to stare at her sharply, all wistfulness gone. "My home?" He locked eyes with her for a moment, sorrow lingering in the forest green depths of his gaze. "Enough discussing. You're needed in the dining hall. I have updated Madame Rose on your progress, and she wishes to speak with you privately. I believe something about your past has intrigued her."

The last thing Cerise wished to do was talk to the insane woman in chains. What was it about her that Madame Rose wished to know? Had she discovered Cerise was a hybrid?

It seemed the other young women hadn't yet, for no one had tried to hurt her. It was common for hybrids to be executed or sent to Denthlire, and since she was already here, an execution seemed more likely. It was dangerous enough already with them knowing that she was a werewolf. People had killed magic-wielders for much less. And if they found out she was part-mage...

She wanted to question Pan further, but Cerise knew she couldn't argue, for her mother's life was at stake. She followed him silently, more afraid than she'd ever admit.

"Cerise!" Madame Rose cheerfully called out, her eyes calmer than usual. Cerise immediately tensed; that could not be a good sign. Raina would often be most quiet before lashing out with a rod, her fists, or magic.

She inched toward her, fighting the urge to shift. It was the worst part of her ability, having to fight the primal urges of the wolf side that always wanted control.

"Madame Rose. Pan said you wished to see me?" Cerise stood ramrod straight, her dark eyes locked with Madame Rose's red-tinged ones.

"Yes, I did indeed. It has been brought to my attention that you're only half-werewolf. I had originally thought that you were just a special werewolf who had control over their shifting. But it seems you are a hybrid, correct?" She chuckled. "My, my, what a shock it is that you're still alive! If I'm correct, your kind is illegal."

Cerise glared at Madame Rose, feeling the blood course hotly through her veins. It had always confused her as a young child when her father would sit her on his knee and explain why she couldn't tell people what her mother could do, or when with her mother, what her father was. It had taken seeing a hybrid burned alive in their house for Cerise to understand how much people feared the mixing of power.

"There's no need to be so angry," Madame Rose continued. "I do not fear you. Allegora has always allowed itself to be ruled by fear and superstition. They fear power especially. Those who might be too powerful, those who might end up finally balancing the scales, those are the ones they torture and subdue beneath them, warping them into the monsters they always feared." Madame Rose licked her lips, the crazy light gleaming once more in her eyes. "They do not understand that they are the monsters.

"If people are scared of those they have twisted and hurt, how much more absolutely twisted and insane are those that inflicted the pain? People are blind!"

Madame Rose's words struck a chord with Cerise. Allegora hated her kind simply because they were afraid. Because the king hated anything out of his control. Because the unknown was terrifying. Oftentimes it wasn't the monsters that needed to be feared, but those who had created them. Maybe Madame Rose wasn't so crazy after all. "Is that the only reason you called me? To ask if it was true that I'm a hybrid?"

Blinking quickly, as if just realizing that Cerise was still in the courtyard, Madame Rose glanced at her. "No, I had another question. If you are indeed a hybrid, then who is your father? It is very rare that a child born from the union of two different species should survive infancy, you know, because your king enjoys murdering children. So, I am curious, what exactly is your father?"

Her father. Cerise gulped, shoving back her panic. That was the other secret she was supposed to keep, no matter what. Hybrids were illegal, but a mage having a child with a werewolf was the highest level of offense. Mages were only supposed to marry within their species or, at worst, with humans.

"He was a human. Because of the weak union between magical and non-magical, it was easier to hide me and my abilities."

Madame Roses sighed softly, her eyes almost sad. "And here I thought that maybe you were a were-mage. Now those are a rare breed. Immensely powerful, too."

Cerise forced an easy smile on her face. "Trust me, if I were a were-mage, I would have been dead a long time ago."

VERRE

VERRE WOULD NEVER admit it, but she missed Baen desperately. She regretted every moment she had not spent by his side. At the time, it hadn't bothered her, but now she might never see him again.

Her jaw clenched as she fought against the thought. She couldn't afford to think negatively; the place was already too depressing as it was.

She turned over on the small and narrow bed, trying to sleep, but her mind wandered again to his deep brown eyes that crinkled when he laughed and that adorable dimple that would form on his chin. Or his smooth olive skin, in blunt contrast to her own creamy white complexion. How he knew when she just needed to be held. No words of advice or comfort, just him stroking her hair, holding her close, and humming softly.

Verre found herself smiling despite efforts to remain serious. She could still remember the first time she had met him. He had been trying to sell one of his inventions to the lords and ladies, hoping one of them would take a fancy to it. That was so like him—caught up in a grand dream that he gave up everything to see come true.

When he had come to their manor to try to sell it to them, Verre had answered his knock. Seeing her, he had nearly dropped the motorized vegetable chopper he was selling. After they were married, he had confessed that he had thought her the most beautiful, fierce person he had ever met. No matter what, he had shared—looking quite embarrassed—he had wanted to make her his new dream and try his hardest to pursue her.

A low chuckle escaped her throat, the small laugh helping her relax. How ever had she attracted such a sociable person?

That first week, he had stopped by three times, selling a different invention each visit. At first, Verre had been annoyed, but his quirky humor finally managed to make her laugh, and she was the sort of person to rarely laugh.

That was when she had known he was special.

He would often remark that when they had walked through the symbolic white ironwood trees together, hand in hand, he had felt like the luckiest, but also most unworthy, man in the world. At that time,

Verre had never thought that she would be blessed with the opportunity to vow that her love to Baen would be as resolute and immortal as the ironwood trees themselves, but here she was, married to him.

That had been astounding. Her? She was nothing but a killer, the only occupation that she had any talent for. She wasn't extremely intelligent, or even beautiful, but Baen had seen something in her, something she didn't see in herself. He saw past the guilt she tried to swallow up in the emptiness of her heart.

Every time he held her close and whispered in her ear that she was the most amazing woman on earth, her heart would pound. She had never seen much worth in herself; she was expendable. Sure, she was talented, but at what? Murder?

But to Baen, she was his world, and he was hers. She was like the sea. Strong. Terrifying. Unpredictable. He was her moon, that unseen force that turned her wild strength into something beautiful.

Baen, her sunshiney jester. Verre clutched the blankets close, tears burning behind her eyes. She swore again that should she escape—when she escaped—she would find another occupation. No more killing. Maybe they could finally swim along the Evanscene shores, and Baen could finally ask the elves the secrets of their metal-working craft.

The thought helped quiet her troubled heart. Taking a deep breath, Verre allowed her mind to still, sleep capturing her faster than she would have thought possible.

It was strange for Verre, waking up to silence. Usually, she would hear Baen's snoring—granted, she found it adorable—or the morning bustle outside the rundown inns she'd usually stay at when on a job. Verre was a silent sleeper, which she attributed to her father, but Baen and her mother made up for it with their booming voices and non-stop prattle.

Rising from the uncomfortable bed, she slipped out of her nightdress and into the tub of cold water she had been provided, beginning what had become her morning routine.

Her skin tightened, and she gasped softly as icy water connected with warm flesh. Ignoring the feeling that she would probably freeze to death, Verre plunged underwater, air bubbles escaping her mouth as she gasped again, this time inhaling water. Coming up coughing, she quickly scrubbed with the lumpy bar of soap to her right and plunged once more beneath the now sudsy water.

Stumbling out as quickly as possible, she grabbed a ragged towel, thin and fraying at the edges, and dried herself off, donning a clean pair of trousers and a grey blouse.

Pan had provided them with many necessities, though Verre preferred to not think about where he had stolen them from. If it had been a stuck-up noble or the royal family, she would be fine with it, but they certainly didn't use ragged towels.

Many nobles thought it was odd that Verre's family fought for the common people and their rights, and that was the very reason they did it. The noblemen didn't see people as all being equals. Her father was fascinated with politics and had many radical ideals about how he believed Allegora should be run.

Of course, her father couldn't always voice his opinions, lest he lose his power to help the people. So, he fought his battles by writing anonymous papers, studying in his library, and distributing food and necessities to those in need.

Verre closed her eyes, almost able to imagine she was in her father's library. She envisioned the heavy curtains draped over the floor-to-ceiling windows, the rich red wood of the floor, and the large bookshelves, each full to bursting with novels, the majority of the bindings worn with use. All was silent but comforting. The smell of old books...

"Verre?" The door opened, and Aura's head popped around the door, the shadows under her eyes indicating a restless night. "Pan is looking for you. We're training again, and he has requested that you teach us all the art of throwing daggers, or in this case, glass shards." Her eyes shifted about, her knuckles white as they clutched the doorframe. Verre had noticed that Aura was always tense, always alert. For the already weakened girl, it must be exhausting, but Aura made no complaint.

She sighed, running a hand through her wet hair, glad for the simplicity of having it cut short. "I'll be there soon. First, I want to grab some food from the dining hall. Perhaps you should rest some more— you don't look fit enough to train. I'm sure Pan will understand."

Despite the fact that Pan was a monster, he seemed concerned for their health, though Verre knew the concern came from his wish for the heist to succeed, not because he actually cared about their welfare. He was complicated. Verre couldn't figure out why he served Madame Rose—what his motive was. All she knew was that he was powerful and extremely dangerous.

"Very well, I'll let him know." Aura scurried out, avoiding Verre's comment about her health. Verre admired the girl's inner strength and determination though she would never state it out loud.

Stepping briskly through the halls, Verre tried to push the silence behind her with each step. It was too hollow, too lonesome, and it only made her miss Baen more.

Thankfully, Madame Rose hadn't called her in today for her "evaluation." Every few days she talked to them one-on-one, supposedly to see how they were coming along, but mostly to just taunt them. It took everything in Verre not to try and kill her.

Entering the dining hall—and noting that the table was overflowing with food for what was likely the last time—Verre grabbed a handful of crescent berries and a leg of some cold hark. Peeling back the berries' skin as she walked toward the ballroom, Verre let her mind wander to the three other young women.

They were all exceptional in their own way; even Verre had to admit that. The gifts they had... it was astounding. She wondered how Madame Rose could even have known about all of them.

It was a question that had bothered her for days now, ever since they had first arrived. Sure, Rose had Pan, but how would he have known where to look? How could he have discovered so much?

Something just didn't add up with Madame Rose, and Verre was going to figure it out. Already, she had a plan for eliminating Pan, but Madame Rose was still an unknown. She would have to tread carefully around her as Verre still wasn't sure what she was capable of.

Her brain began to run through all possible means of escape. She could torture Pan into teleporting her away, but his healing abilities would make torture rather ineffective. With a frown, she shook her head. Yes, it would be too difficult. Besides, she couldn't bind him.

Verre growled and threw a glass shard into the ground, shattering it. He was complicating everything!

Would the other girls be able to help her escape? She snorted with laughter at the thought. It was a wonder Aura was even still alive, and Cerise seemed competent, but werewolves had a tendency to be unpredictable. And Blanca? Well, she might be powerful, but she had absolutely no idea how to use that to her advantage. It was a miracle she hadn't died yet either.

Verre was on her own with this. A slight twinge of guilt settled in her stomach, but she brushed it aside. It wasn't her job to make sure they all survived. She hadn't gotten them into this, and she didn't have to get them out.

An idea dawned on her, and she quickened her pace, heading away from the ballroom. The grey walls all began to blur together as she lengthened her stride, practically running. There it was. Verre came to a quick stop, swallowing back the fear that crept up her throat.

The castle doors.

Pan had warned them of the dangers of Denthlire, but maybe the only way to escape was to leave the safety of the castle's stone walls.

Cursing the slight tremble of her fingers, she inched the heavy door open, a stale breeze bringing with it the smell of death.

It was much darker than she expected. At least it lived up to its name, for fog filled the air above, and smoke wafted up from the ground. The shrieking was even more piercing out here, and Verre tensed, a glass spear clenched tightly in her fist.

A shape came swirling out of the smoke, followed by another... and another. Verre started to take a cautious step back, then froze.

The shapes were crying.

"Help us," one whimpered. "It burns. Oh, it burns."

Another began to wail, the sound becoming the shriek Verre had grown so accustomed to. "Where's my mama?"

Nausea came over Verre so strong that she could feel bile burning in her throat.

They were children.

The shapes scrambled even closer, their forms flickering. The ground hissed and smoked as they drew near, and the children began to glow.

Whatever they were, they weren't children anymore. At least not living ones. Verre stumbled back, slamming the door shut behind her.

Slumping to the ground, she covered her ears with her hands, unable to bear the sound of crying.

Now she understood why Pan refused to leave the castle.

BLANCA

NOT BEING ABLE to speak should have bothered Blanca more. From a young age, she had learned that it was often best to keep her opinions to herself. No one got angry if she kept quiet. Now, instead of getting hurt for talking, she hurt others.

But she never would. Even the thought of inflicting pain on another person turned her stomach to knots. She would never be like her father. But… now she could make him pay for what he had done.

If only he was here. She could say whatever she wanted. She could scream whatever she wanted, and he wouldn't be able to hurt her. He couldn't leave any scars.

Shame engulfed her. What would Lyra say about these thoughts? She'd be appalled. Blanca was appalled at herself too. Those were thoughts of a monster. And she refused to be one.

Wandering through another courtyard, this one thankfully lacking Madame Rose, Blanca realized that this place was beautiful, in its own way, and that it might have actually been relaxing if it weren't for the fact that she had survived one monster only to be captured by another.

While her past was still in fragments, she did know that the unusual fascinated her. So while Denthlire frightened some, she found it more intriguing than terrifying once she had accepted her fate here.

It was a new world to discover. And she was nearly invincible when she spoke, for there was hardly any living thing that didn't breathe air. It was strange, knowing she had a way to protect herself. She wasn't used to that.

Studying the engravings that seemed to be everywhere, an image of a young infant caught her eye, and she winced, putting a hand out to steady herself.

It had been an icy fall day. The dry wind swept through the land, freezing all whose flesh it touched. The low cries of a woman could be heard down the hall of the manor, even from the outer parlor where Blanca huddled, drawing her blanket as close as possible. She had never imagined that giving birth would be so painful for Lyra.

Flames flickered in the hearth, casting dancing shadows upon the gleaming wooden walls. Blanca tried to block out Lyra's moans of pain, but then she heard a sound that sent a dagger of fear shooting through her heart. It was laughter. Harsh, raucous laughter that reverberated through the first floor. It was her father. He never laughed, except when he drank.

Of course he would be drinking while Lyra gave birth. He hated children ever since the king had poisoned his mind with power and magic. He hated Blanca, reminding her often that she was the reason her mother was dead. He had once told her that she had been a mistake, that her mother wasn't supposed to have gotten pregnant.

When he had found out that Lyra was pregnant, he had thrown a fit, ranting about how they could not afford to feed another mouth, even though he was one of the wealthiest lords in Allegora.

Blanca could still hear the shattering glass, the angry shouts that made her want to flee from it all, to escape to the calm and peaceful woods. If he was drinking now, she feared that he might try to harm Lyra or the baby. He was not a sane man when he drank, if he were ever sane at all.

Crawling out from underneath the comfort of the heavy wool blanket, she hurried up the staircase, afraid for Lyra's wellbeing. It was easy to follow the sounds of labored breathing and hoarse cries. Blanca wove through the halls, finding Lyra and several of the maids in one of the guest bedrooms.

Lyra glanced up, her eyes wide in surprise, her face flushed with sweat and exertion. "Blanca? You shouldn't be here. Your father—" She arched her back, her jaw clenched tightly as she battled the contraction. Lyra was always so strong and *brilliant; it was frightening to see her in so much pain and to be helpless. Loud steps echoed on the staircase and slurred mumbling followed. Lyra paled even further, her face set with determination.*

"Blanca, I need you to bolt the door. Hala, please pick up the knife to your right. If Rikor tries to enter, we need to make sure this child survives, understood?" Blanca nodded, knowing she should be terrified. But the thought of Lyra or the baby being hurt set aflame something within her. If she didn't help, who knew what her father might do? Hala picked up the knife as Blanca bolted the door, hands shaking.

The steps came closer, echoing ominously as they stopped in front of the bedroom door. Loud, sloppy knocking followed. "Lyra? Lyra! Open this door! What did I say about children? We can't afford them—didn't I say we can't afford them? I've counted all my coin a hundred times over; I'm the wealthiest lord in the land. Children," he snorted in disgust, his words slurred by alcohol, banging once more. "They're not worth it! Now open this door so I can fix everything. I'll buy you a pretty wand that will make your ballgowns change colors with just a flick of your hand. Doesn't that sound better?"

It was always drink with him. It warped his mind, making him spew silly, nonsensical things like not being able to afford children. But it was terrifying since Blanca knew that some part of him truly believed that. The part of him the king had created.

Lyra glared fiercely at Blanca and shook her head. "Do not let him in." She rested her head back, gathering herself to push.

135

Blanca watched in fascination as Lyra proceeded to deliver the baby, a ragged scream tearing from her lips. Her father pounded again, the sound of a bottle being thrown following. Blanca flinched but didn't move. She knew what he would do if he entered. She glanced down at the scars on her arms. He was a monster.

A small whimper called from the arms of another one of the maids, who beamed happily. "Lady Lyra, you have a beautiful new daughter."

Lyra panted heavily, ignoring the questioning shouts from outside the door. "She is beautiful, very much like her sister." She embraced the tiny infant, pride gleaming in her eyes. "My Crescent Rose."

Crescent Rose. So that was her full name. The memory left Blanca anguished, tears welling up in her eyes. She still could not remember what happened after she had escaped with little Rose, where they had gone.

It still felt strange to know that she had died. Randune had said there had been an apple beside her, a poisoned one. Why had she eaten it? Was it possible that it had been of her own free will? But what had happened to Rose? She clutched her head, a headache pounding at her skull.

Who would know that information?

Blanca lifted her head, her mind clearing. Of course, Madame Rose. She had stated Rose's name and said that Pan would kill her if Blanca was not obedient. She must know where Rose was. The thought of finally knowing after weeks of turmoil sent joy shooting through her veins. Rose must still be alive.

She turned right, making her way down a long corridor. After a week, even the labyrinth-like castle halls were familiar. Mandatory visits with Madame Rose had taught all of them the way to her courtyard, and Blanca maneuvered that way with hardly a thought.

During the visits, Pan always forced Blanca to stand at least twenty feet away when speaking with Madame Rose. Now, a dangerous thrill ran though Blanca, realizing her poison must scare them both. She knew firsthand the power fear could wield over someone.

Her mind and heart still bore the traces of the fear, determination, and pride from the memory. She loved Lyra and Rose, and now they were gone. She had to get answers.

"Blanca!" Madame Rose didn't bother hiding her surprise and confusion as Blanca marched into the courtyard. "What brings you here?" Her chains rattled slightly as she stood straighter. "I must say, I wasn't expecting you. Cerise, perhaps, or even Verre, but not you."

Blanca strode forward, for a moment relishing the force and fear with which Madame Rose strove to back up. How dare this woman threaten an infant, her sister, and be completely fine with it? Had she captured her?

The thought angered Blanca, poison beginning to seep from her skin. "Where is she?"

Madame Rose's eyes widened with fright, her narrow frame heaving with panic. Her wrists jerked clumsily against her shackles, leaving fresh bloodstains over the rusty old ones. "Where is who? Blanca, dear, you must be more specific."

She growled in frustration. This woman was maddening! More poison oozed from her pores, dripping to the stone floor below. For a moment, she allowed herself to glance down at her hands, marveling at the sticky green substance that now coated them. Was this the same poison that came from her lungs? The smell was acidic, making Blanca wrinkle her nose. The rattle of the chains again brought her focus back to Madame Rose.

"Where is Rose, my sister? You know where she is." At Madame Rose's silence, she screamed, deafening and raw. "Tell me!" Poison spewed out of her mouth, winding its way toward Madame Rose.

Panic welled up inside of her, afraid of what Madame Rose's answer might be.

"Fine! Fine, I concede," Madame Rose shouted, her wrists and ankles rubbed raw. "I will tell you where she is on one condition. Should you refuse, I will have Pan kill both Rose and Lyra immediately."

Blanca shut her mouth, the remaining poison wandering lazily about before sinking into the ground.

Her body trembled as she realized that she just might have spelled the deaths of both Lyra and Rose by her hasty and foolish act. What had she been thinking?

She hadn't been thinking at all. She had let a terrifying rage consume her. Hands shaking, she said, "Very well. What is your condition?"

Madame Rose smiled, the blood from her wrists staining her faded gown as the wounds healed. "My condition is this: when your mission is complete, and the slippers rest in Pan's hands, you must eliminate the other three. Use your poison and kill them all, every last one. Should you fail, I will make sure you personally witness the dying screams of your family. Agreed? Once you have completed this, I will tell you anything you wish."

Blanca gulped. Kill them? In cold blood?

The thought was nauseating. The other women were more or less kind to her, helping her to improve in her training, especially Cerise.

Blanca was not a killer, not even a fighter. How could she just kill them? But then she thought of Lyra and little Rose. Madame Rose would be sure to torture them slowly; she would revel in their pain. Blanca closed her eyes and nodded slowly.

"Agreed."

16

AURA

AURA STILL COULDN'T believe that it was possible to have this much food. It always filled the table, and not even just simple foods, but rich meats, hearty vegetables, and delicious drinks.

It was her first instinct to eat as much as she could as fast as she could, but she learned quickly that was not necessary. For what seemed like the hundredth time, Aura wished that Aerik and Aela were here eating this delicious food with her, growing strong and healthy.

"Ladies, your attention, please." Pan rose from where he had been lounging against the wall. The candles illuminated his face, accentuating the sharp cut of his jaw.

Aura could not decide how old he looked. From his bright red hair and youthful body, she would have assumed that he was in his mid-twenties, but his eyes spoke differently. The forest green held far too much wisdom, far too much pain. But there was this incredible coldness to them as well, a coldness that made Aura want to avert her eyes.

"You have trained for just over a week now. Your progress has been noted and reported to Madame Rose. She is most pleased. Tomorrow I will be transporting you all to Allegora, where you will then be given further instructions."

Suddenly, Aura's food was no longer appetizing. For some reason, she had allowed herself to believe that they wouldn't actually have to do anything. That they would eat well, train their minds and bodies a bit, and then be done with this bizarre adventure.

It had been a foolish hope, a silly one in fact. Glancing around at the other faces at the table, Aura saw that she wasn't the only one to lose her will to eat. Blanca especially seemed frightened.

"Will we have to collect provisions beforehand?" came Verre's calm question. How she managed to remain so collected during such a terrifying moment was beyond Aura. The odds of them all being brutally executed by the royal family for treason were exceedingly high, and that was if some deadly magical creature didn't kill them first.

But Aura would risk the chance of dying if it meant that Aela and Aerik would be safe.

"Yes, prepare as best as possible. I will make one last supply run before we leave tomorrow. Any weapon preferences? Excluding Verre, of course."

Verre smirked and nodded in agreement.

A weapon? Aura didn't know what to say as weapons were illegal in Oobay. Of course, that hadn't stopped gangs from creating weapons from anything they could find, and, if nothing else, their fists. "A dagger, if you can find one." Daggers, a useful and generic weapon. She couldn't go wrong with one, right?

Cerise quickly asked for a double-bladed ax.

Blanca hesitated, finally answering quietly, "A bow."

Aura was surprised. Did Blanca know how to use one? She was a noble, and they usually knew very little about weaponry, especially the women.

As if noticing everyone's confusion and surprise, Blanca quickly explained. "I always wanted to be skilled in some form of combat, and archery was the only one my father deemed lady-like enough. I'm a pretty decent shot."

Everyone leaned back as she spoke, afraid of the poison. Blanca blushed and shut her mouth, the poison fading away.

The weapons sorted out, Aura pushed away from the table, anxiety gnawing at her insides. She needed to be alone so she could sort out her emotions. All of this was coming to a head far too quickly, and the tears behind her eyes wanted nothing more than to be released. The more she walked, the more they burned at her eyes, until everything was a blur.

Collapsing down onto her bed—miserably noting that it seemed lumpier than usual—she allowed her body to relax, and so the tears began to fall.

Aura was scared. It wasn't supposed to have been like this, none of it was. She wasn't supposed to be a mother to her two younger siblings or steal a powerful magical item just so they wouldn't be murdered. She was supposed to be learning the history of Allegora or discussing the lore behind the stars in the sky. Her parents were supposed to be there, in Oobay, taking care of her as well as her siblings.

But they weren't, and they never would be. It was up to Aura to protect her siblings, and if it meant dying, so be it.

Taking deep, shuddering breaths, Aura slowly relaxed, trying to will her body to sleep well one last time.

———◆———

After reasoning with herself for a great length of time, Aura finally felt composed. Her fear was locked away, and she wasn't going to dwell on it, couldn't dwell on it. Fear was just another obstacle that would keep her from her family.

A dagger was resting just inside her room when she awoke. Aura stole glances at it as she changed clothes, pulling her leather boots up to her knees.

It had a foot-long, straight blade, the metal gleaming in the low light. The hilt was wrapped in what appeared to be dragon skin, glowing a faint blue. It had no crossguard, but the blade had intricate carvings engraved into it. Whoever had owned this sword before Aura must have been a lucky person indeed. Lucky and wealthy.

She grinned as she gripped it, marveling at the ridged sheerness of the dragon skin. It awed her to think that a dragon had at one point shed that very skin.

Her amazement was interrupted as reality took hold once more. She had a mission to accomplish, and daydreaming about dragons wasn't going to secure Aela and Aerik's safety. Taking a few deep breaths to calm her nerves, Aura strode out of her room, almost tripping because of the heaviness of her boots. It was odd to be wearing such quality apparel. Back in Oobay, she had been lucky to have owned a pair of tattered shoes that were more patches of dirty cloth than leather.

Stopping to inspect herself in an elaborate but tarnished mirror, she couldn't help but admire the costliness of her clothing. Aura didn't even care about how he had procured the items, for they were now hers. Her hands slid along the heavy wool of her trousers, marveling at the warmth of her skin. The linen blouse hung loose on her thin frame, the neutral grey the perfect color.

As she continued to walk, Aura couldn't help but grin at the dignified click of her boots as it echoed through the hall. How sophisticated, how important. How odd to feel powerful.

The ballroom was eerily silent, despite the fact that it held five people. Glancing around at the pensive faces, Aura stilled her own tongue. Now was not the time to speak. Pan glanced over the four of them, looking impressive in his black leather attire, twin glittering swords peeking out from behind his broad shoulders.

"M'ladies, friends, and associates of Madame Rose," he began, earning glares from both Aura and Cerise. "The time has come to complete your mission. Dorthea's slippers are hidden deep within the Bluefrost Mountains, veiled from sight and touch by countless mage spells. Unfortunately, I am unaware of its exact location. There are strong magical shields hiding it from me, so you are on your own. Don't underestimate the magic guarding it or the king's own cruelty."

Aura tensed, knowing just enough about magic and the king to fear both.

Verre spoke up, her tone confused. "The slippers are on a mountain? Not a vault or the palace?"

"Yes, a mountain." Pan held Verre's gaze for a second before dropping his eyes and continuing. "We will arrive at the foothills of the Bluefrost Mountains. I will have to leave you at that point, though I will observe from afar. Like I said, from there you will be on your own; I have no other information to give." Pan shouldered a pack of provisions as he finished.

Stunned silence followed. That was it? Surely Pan had discovered more information than just the slippers' whereabouts?

Cerise was the one to voice their concerns. "That's it? We're risking our very lives and the lives of our loved ones for a vague idea of its location and the warning of magic?"

Pan sighed. "I know it's not ideal—"

"Ideal? Ideal! This is a far cry from ideal! We could all be blasted to smithereens, vaporized to nothing, or turned into a flock of crows. Mage magic is tricky business and extremely difficult to detect." Cerise was seething, her fists clenched and her breath coming in rapid bursts. "You should have been better prepared."

Pan crossed the room, slamming Cerise against the wall of the ballroom, the ancient chandeliers shaking and shuddering above. "I will not tolerate such insolence, little wolf."

Cerise snarled, a deep-throated noise that sent a shiver down Aura's spine. The air was thick with tension, so palpable Aura could almost feel it run along her skin. Pan's next words made her skin freeze.

"But no need to worry your curly head about it. I know your secret even if your companions don't."

He laughed at Cerise's astonished look. "What? You think I believed your lie? Dear Cerise, you're going to have to learn that no one keeps anything from Madame Rose. I'm sure your magic will be quite helpful."

Aura was confused. What did Pan mean? Did Cerise have magical abilities they weren't aware of?

She had seen the posters people had pasted on door-frames, the ones that hurled insults at magic-wielders who were illegal simply by being born. Aura remembered having to cover Aerik's eyes so he wouldn't read the horrific things people wrote. So if Cerise was hiding magic, it would make sense. Allegora was not kind to people like them. Aura knew firsthand.

"What?" Blanca whispered, eyes fearful. "What is he talking about?"

Cerise squirmed out of Pan's grasp, her neck red. "He's lying! Why should we believe anything he says? He's just trying to cause division. Our main priority right now is to save our families."

Verre nodded curtly. "Agreed. We have no time for emotional outbursts. Right now we have a mission," her lips curled in distaste, "and we need to all work together. Is that understood?"

Verre looked like the leader they needed—fearless, confident, and cunning. Aura felt a little safer knowing she was going with them.

"I agree," Aura declared, garnering a nod from Cerise. They all looked to Blanca who had yet to say anything more. Her look was one of distrust.

"Very well. Agreed." The words were cautious.

Pan smiled. "Excellent! Team spirit is always a necessity on a mission. Make sure to grab your packs before I teleport us away."

Aura snatched her pack, making sure her sword was secure. They all grasped a part of Pan, be it an arm or his tunic. She closed her eyes as the feeling of weightlessness took over.

It was freezing.

She opened her eyes to wisps of purple and blue, but everything was a haze. A second more and there was brightness, a brilliant blue light. Blinking furiously, Aura took inventory of where she was, and her jaw dropped. There was snow everywhere, sparkling, pure white snow. She stooped to brush her fingers over it, marveling at its frigidness.

"Welcome, m'ladies," Pan gestured to the snow, "to the foothills of the Bluefrost Mountains."

CERISE

THE BLUEFROST MOUNTAINS were much colder than Cerise had anticipated. The chill drove straight to her bones, making her shiver. She was accustomed to the mild climate of Lithrium. Cerise longed to shift, to be blanketed by her wolf's thick coat of fur, but now was not the time.

"As you can see, it is quite cold here. Unfortunately, it will only get colder the higher you venture." Pan gestured upward, Cerise's eyes following, fastening on the massive heaps of snow and stone. She gulped, realizing how truly enormous the mountains were. How were they supposed to find the slippers?

A more chilling thought invaded her mind. How were they supposed to steer clear of the spells Pan had talked about? There was far too much land to cover and not enough resources or time.

"You each have enough food and water to last a week, but the temperatures will kill you long before then if you're not careful. These mountains have a way of dropping to temperatures so cold that even the goils—wily, scaly creatures with a love for precious jewels and stew; nasty beasts, actually—seek shelter in their caves. Hopefully, you won't have to experience that, for then I would have the grueling task of finding others to do this job." He glared sternly at the four of them as if it was their fault they had been kidnapped and forced to steal a pair of slippers.

"Do you think we'll *all* survive?" Aura asked, clutching her arms close to her chest in a attempt to stay warm. Cerise pitied her, pitied them all. Even with the thick clothing they wore, the cold still managed to seep through.

"Most likely not, but you each have gifts that will help you succeed," Pan said. "Now, just be smart. Keep your wits about you and you'll do fine. All you must do is call my name when you're done; I will be there." His eyes scanned the mountainside quickly before coming back to rest on the group. "Well, I must be off." With that, he vanished, leaving only a faint wisp of purple behind.

Cerise stood in stunned silence for a moment, the realization of what they were required to do finally hitting her.

"Very well, let's find shelter," Verre said. "We have one week, if we're smart, and already the day is nearly halfway done. Once we've found shelter, we can take stock of what we have."

All three turned to Verre, who shouldered her pack confidently, her eyes darting about. "A cave would work best if we can find one."

No one argued with her, Cerise secretly relieved that she wouldn't have to give any orders herself. Verre was the most capable of the four. Still, it stung a little that everyone gravitated toward the tall woman. The wolf within her wanted to be the alpha of the group, while the human in her knew it was smart for Verre to take charge.

"We should make sure to stick together too. We're unfamiliar with the terrain," Cerise suggested, thankful—for once—for the survival skills Raina had taught her through her abuse and neglect.

Verre seemed almost surprised at her knowledge—as if she hadn't expected any of them to be competent.

"Correct. Until we have any sort of idea of what's going on, we must stick together. A week is an extremely short amount of time to both adjust and find the slippers, so I have a plan. We're going to stay longer than a week, but in order to do that, we need to find a source of fresh water and food soon."

It was a solid plan. They hadn't been given a deadline, only one for how long their provisions would last.

A chilling wind blew through, turning Cerise's blood to ice. Her vision went blurry, and all she could hear was the thunder of her heartbeat. Verre's voice faded to a dull roar, and her brain could only focus on the thought of warmth. She had to get warm.

Bones snapped loudly, and her body was instantly warmer as thick fur crept over her skin, ending at the points of her ears. Her vision swam for a moment.

She had shifted. It had happened in the blink of an eye, and she fought to keep her head clear.

Kill.

She shook her large head, a low growl making its way up her throat.

No.

The thought had such force behind it that the bloodlust running through her brain faded into the background, her thoughts clearing. She was in control.

Muscles rippled just beneath her skin, her senses amplified. Shame filled her as she realized that she had shifted accidentally, like some frightened pup. If she hadn't gained control, who knew what might have happened?

Cerise trotted towards Verre slowly, preferring to not be impaled by a fragment of glass. Verre stepped back, her eyes suspicious, glass shards gripped tightly in either hand. "Cerise?"

She nodded, allowing her nose to evaluate the scents around her. Verre's was of faint blood, sweat, and basil. Blanca smelled the best, of cinnamon and all manner of spices. It saturated the girl's very pores.

Cerise wrinkled her snout at the smell of Aura. Oil. Hot oil, rotting wood, and dust. But there was a faint smell of citrus as well. Cerise stored these scents in her brain so that she would always be able to track them should she need to. Then she picked out the smell of water, pure and fresh. It was closer than she would have guessed.

Ears perked, she loped toward the smell.

Verre motioned the others to follow as well, grabbing Cerise's pack. The wolf followed the smell, winding carefully through the snow, her body perfect for slicing through it with ease. Stopping at a small mound of snow, she began to dig furiously, unearthing a small stream that was mostly frozen.

"Nice work!" Verre exclaimed, crouching next to Cerise. "Aura, can I see your dagger?" Aura blinked in surprise, her hand curling around the hilt defensively.

"I'm not going to break it," Verre said, rolling her eyes. "I need it to break the ice. The blade is kirium, the most durable of metals." Aura reluctantly handed it over, her eyes fastened on Cerise.

A few well-aimed blows were all it took to get the stream flowing again. "This looks like it could be a steady source of water for us. Now, we must find a shelter. Finding food will be easier, especially with Cerise."

Cerise snorted, tossing her large head. While it felt good to have control over wolf form, she wasn't pleased with Verre taking control of everything. It was probably the werewolf instincts trying to take over again. She wanted to be the pack leader. But the human side of her knew that Verre was much more capable of leading even though the thought made her want to growl.

"I spotted a rock formation on our way here. Perhaps there was a cave?" Aura said, biting her lip as she rubbed her arms again. Aura had said she was from Oobay, a city known for its oppressive heat. Considering that, Aura must have been freezing, having never experienced cold like this.

"Maybe there was. We must hurry, for the sun sets much sooner in the mountains." Verre rose and set out the way they had come. Cerise rose as well, noting a rotting stump just a few yards to her left. It would not be wise to forget where such a good source of water was. Satisfied that she would remember, Cerise trotted after them, hopeful that they would find a place to rest.

"Yes, this should work." Verre stood inside the cave, a smile on her face. Glancing around, Cerise noticed that it was a small cave, only ten times her length long and four times her length wide. Still, smaller meant warmer. The familiar scent of musty darkness, so similar to her cave back in Lithrium, comforted her.

Blanca wrinkled her nose as she examined the wet and dirty cave. "Will it be warm enough in here to survive the night? Won't a fire simply suffocate us as well?" The words were spoken in a whisper, but everyone stepped back like usual.

They were intelligent questions, but Cerise couldn't help but feel like Blanca just wanted an excuse to not sleep in such a dirty place. She was a noble; why wouldn't she be concerned with such trivial things? Cerise knew it wasn't fair, but it was people like Blanca that had made people like her illegal.

"With all of us combined, it will get plenty warm in here. As for the fire, we'll only create one at the mouth of the cave. That way it can frighten away any creatures and also prevent us from suffocating, as you said." The tone in Verre's voice was final, and no one complained when she began to unpack their satchels and clean the cave.

Cerise wished to shift back, but because of her rather messy shift earlier, she hadn't had time to step out of her clothes. It would be humiliating to be naked in front of women who were practically strangers. She couldn't voice her concerns, though, so either she remained a wolf or dealt with the embarrassment. She decided on the latter.

The sound of bones snapping attracted everyone's attention, but it was too late to stop shifting. Once fully human, Cerise reached for her pack, only to discover that she had clothing on, the same clothes she had worn before she shifted. Puzzled, she sat down, examining the fabric. Had it shifted with her?

A spell of bending.

Cerise backed up, her heart pounding. How had she known that? Why did she know that? What was happening?

"Cerise? Are you alright?" Aura's concerned face came into focus. Her question took a moment to process. Alright? No, she was most definitely not alright. Was this what Pan had meant? Had she just understood a spell? The thought was alarming. If what she thought was true, then that meant that the mage blood that flowed through her veins was not diluted by the blood of her mother.

She could perform magic.

The notion was dizzying.

"Cerise! What's wrong?" Verre's sharp voice brought her mind speeding back. Glancing around, she saw everyone's confused and worried faces. They didn't understand the significance of shifting with clothing, which she was immensely thankful for.

"Oh, me? I'm fine. Just a little dizzy after shifting, that's all," Cerise lied, unable to tell them yet. What would they do if they knew? Mages were frightening enough on their own, but a were-mage? Blanca would most likely poison her on the spot.

But how had Pan known?

That was something she'd have to figure out later. Only one thing was certain right now—she had to keep her new-found ability a secret.

18

VERRE

THOUGH SHE PREFERRED to work alone, Verre had to admit that she enjoyed being the leader of a group. It came naturally to her, coming up with a plan and making sure others followed it the same as herself. It was a position that she was far more comfortable with than she cared to acknowledge.

Rising from the painful rock floor, she observed that everyone was still sleeping except for Aura, who crouched at the mouth of the cave. Stepping carefully around the packs and sleeping bodies, Verre came to sit next to her. "Couldn't sleep?"

Aura jumped, hand on her dagger.

"Easy there, it's just me." Verre rolled her eyes and grinned. "But nice reflexes."

Aura's hand dropped, her pale face easily flaming with embarrassment. The morning was frigid, Verre's breath turning to fog even so close to the dwindling fire. Heaping some more sticks onto it and hoping that the dryads wouldn't be too angry—if the branches were in fact from a sentient tree—she looked out over the mountainside.

It was truly beautiful up here, especially as the sun just began to hit the snow, sending radiant sparkles glimmering for miles. It was so quiet, so peaceful.

Perhaps she and Baen could one day visit the Bluefrost Mountains at a time where there was no danger. He would probably end up finding some new way of traveling over the snow. That's how Baen's mind worked. Everything could be made easier with technology. In a world filled with magic—whether it was well-received or not—he had found a way to compete with the convenience magic brought: inventing.

Verre, on the other hand, was content with what she knew. Unknowns held danger, something she couldn't prepare for. The future itself was nebulous, a fact that scared her. She felt secure when she knew the facts, when she had everything under control.

Baen loved the unknown, saying it was one of the many joys of life. He would often wake her up in the middle of the night and demand that she follow him. Laughing, she always did. He would then drag her outside to watch the stars, always talking on and on about the constellations and the fact that hardly anything was known about the space that surrounded them. He made the unknown seem exciting, breathtaking even.

"Verre? What are you thinking about?" As if realizing the bluntness of what she had said, Aura hastily added, "You're smiling. Are you thinking about your family?"

With a pang of guilt, Verre realized she hadn't thought of her parents, not in a while. "Sort of. I was thinking of my husband, Baen. I miss him so much." Her voice failed her and caught slightly. Verre quickly glanced over at Aura, gauging her response to see if she should continue.

"Baen? What an interesting name." Aura grinned. "What does he look like? Is he tall and dreamy?"

Verre laughed, able to picture Baen's response: *Me? Dreamy? Darling, I'm gorgeous.*

"Yes, he's both tall and dreamy, though I'm an inch taller, a fact he's still bothered by. He's also an inventor."

"He sounds wonderful. How long have you been married? And what does he look like?" Aura sat up a little straighter, her eyes bright with curiosity.

Was it dangerous for Verre to discuss all of this with her? The girl was only sixteen, after all. Besides, she needed to know that Aura could be trusted. But that didn't mean the facts she told her had to be true.

"We've been married a few months now. Neither one of us had any idea what we were doing, only that we wanted to spend the rest of our lives together." Verre sighed, a smile tugging at the corners of her lips.

That had been the most amazing yet nerve-wracking day of her life. He was her moon, lighting up the world she believed to be so dark.

"You sound like you're head-over-heels in love," Aura teased. "Who would have thought that you of all people would be married. The hardened, no-nonsense, warrior type."

It was true—she was the last person people expected to have a husband, and a great one at that. Well, life was full of the unknowns Baen was so fond of.

Perhaps their love was another one of those surprises that no one prepared for. And when she thought of it like that, she realized that maybe the unknown wasn't quite so frightening after all. "Yes, I love him more than anyone in the world," she said softly.

Aura nodded, her eyes sad. "My parents were like that, acting like young lovers instead of mature adults who had children. They didn't care what others thought of them or who saw them kiss. It was pretty funny, actually." Her voice quieted. "But that was a long time ago. They're both gone now."

Verre studied the young woman, whose eyes and frame spoke of hardship and who was being far too vulnerable to a killer. She had only been to Oobay once and had vowed to never return, not unless she had an army to burn those horrid factories to the ground.

Rage blossomed in her chest, burning so hot that Verre feared it might spill out in her speech. There were better ways of creating the mages' magical items, ways that didn't involve people, children, dying every day. Somehow, Aura had managed to endure sixteen years there, and apparently, her siblings had too. She was a survivor.

"What happened to them?" Verre knew that many times it wasn't the adults and teenagers that died, but the children. The others were the ones who were shipped away to the mines and palace.

The palace.

Verre shuddered at the thought, knowing full well how despicable the place truly was.

"No. My mother was sent to the palace, and my father is imprisoned in a factory, forced to work day and night until he dies. He tried to steal medicine for my sister." Aura said it without emotion, as if every tear and angry scream had already been used up. She should have been choked up, trying to hold back tears.

Being sent to the palace was a death sentence, and no one lasted long in the factories. Verre would have murdered people for what they had done if those had been her parents. She couldn't understand why Aura was so calm.

Indignation simmered inside Verre at the thought. Unable to keep her anger in check, she said, "Why haven't you gotten revenge? Killed those who hurt your parents? Your ability is perfectly suited to it. Doesn't it still hurt?" Verre was furious just thinking about it. Where was the justice?

"Of course it still hurts!" Aura's voice cracked, eyes shining. Regret twinged in Verre's stomach and she wondered if the topic was too sensitive. Why in all of Denthlire did she have to go and be sympathetic? She must be growing soft around all these children.

"And yes, I have wondered if it would help the pain at all if I avenged my parents by killing the people who did this. Sometimes I wonder if it would have changed anything.

"But if there's one thing my parents taught me, it's that revenge should never be an option. It will never satisfy you. We should choose to think better of others, despite how evil they may be. It's hard to not let bitterness take control," Aura blinked back tears, "but revenge is not an option for me and never will be."

Guilt washed over Verre. She had always been obsessed with revenge, making sure people got what they deserved. She had always defended it, calling it justice. Was it just revenge? Horrible, burning-hot revenge? The thought was humbling, humiliating even.

"I'm sorry. I spoke in haste. You're right, revenge is wrong, but getting justice for what happened to your parents is right, is it not?" This conversation had gotten too deep for Verre's comfort, so she tried to steer it toward a safe ending.

Aura shook her head slowly. "There's nothing wrong with justice, but it would be revenge for me. I couldn't be objective about it. I would want them to suffer for what they had done; I would go too far. I can't allow myself to seek revenge in the name of justice."

Seeking revenge in the name of justice. That struck Verre deep. Deeper than she cared to admit.

The memory of Prince Jonad's death washed over her. That had been revenge in the name of justice.

She remembered playing with Jonad when they were little, some people having even thought they would wed eventually. She remembered thinking it odd that a boy so much older would take a fancy to her. She also remembered not knowing that just because he was the prince, he did not have permission to touch her.

Once the nightmares started, she'd wake up screaming his name. Then her parents finally forbid him from visiting, much to the king's displeasure.

"That is wise to be able to discern the difference between revenge and justice," Verre said quietly.

"Thank you. My mother made sure that she taught us all well. She would never tolerate disrespect, but was still the easiest person to talk to. In a lot of ways, she was the rock of our family." Aura crossed her arms, bringing Verre's attention to the cold. It must be starting to affect Aura, but since she didn't complain, Verre let her continue. It was clear that the girl had a lot of pent-up emotion that needed to be released. Verre just happened to, unfortunately, be the one she vented to.

"You see, she wasn't born in Oobay, or anywhere in Allegora. She came from Evanscene, where her family had lived by the sea. Her parents were fishermen, trading with the elves that lived on the coast. Being a wanderer, she left Evanscene and traveled to many other lands in Atulau. She visited the dwarves of Moorehaven but fell in love with Allegora. There she met my father.

"They were both poor and had been promised good wages in Oobay. They never left," she said sadly. "I wish to travel like she did, someday. I especially want to find Ookramok." Her eyes lit up with excitement, her tone dropping in awe as she spoke.

Ookramok, Moorehaven, Evanscene. They were all places Verre had heard of, but Allegorians rarely traveled anymore. The king opposed it.

No one had ever traveled to Ookramok and lived to tell the tale. Supposedly, it was the land of the Ancient Ones, the dragons. A land filled with mystery and magic.

"You believe Ookramok exists? Did your mother ever visit it?" Baen would have been so excited to hear that someone had been to the other lands of Atalau. He had always wanted to visit them, saying that the tools of Moorehaven were unparalleled, as was the beauty of Evanscene.

"No, but she did see a dragon. A magnificent gold one whose wings seemed to graze the edges of the sky and whose eyes shone like fiery stars. That's what solidified her belief that Ookramok must be real—that it was where all the dragons had fled to when humankind took control." Aura got a dreamy look in her eyes, as if she could picture the golden beast.

Verre had to admit that the thought of a dragon was electrifying. They were supposedly every color imaginable: deep sea green, vibrant blue, blood red, bright gold, shimmering silver... They sounded beautifully terrible, like a raging storm. "It must have been an incredible sight."

"Indeed." Aura lost focus, squinting out past the cave entrance and frowning. "What is that flying toward us?" She rose slowly, eyes straining.

Verre leapt up herself, prepared for the worst, her eyes picking up on the rapidly approaching object.

It was… "Baen?"

19

BLANCA

THE SNOW-COVERED TREES that filled the mountainside reminded Blanca of the forest behind her father's manor. She half-expected a dryad to materialize out of the birch to her left and wave cheerily. Wrapping her arms tightly around her waist, she sighed, the sight making her homesick.

Worry gnawed at her insides—time was running out. She would have to kill them soon. How she wished they wouldn't even find the slippers. Then she would be the one to die, hopefully.

The more she thought about it, the more nausea threatened to empty the contents of her stomach. How could she kill them? Blanca took another deep breath, steadying her pounding heart.

She would kill them all, every last one. She had to. Even the new man who had joined them, the handsome one who had somehow gotten Verre to cry and hold him close.

Baen, he had said his name was. Blanca snuck a glance at the two of them snuggled together under a woolen blanket. Verre almost looked happy. Guilt squirmed inside of Blanca, knowing that she would rip that happiness away soon. She had never pictured Verre as one to marry, but apparently, she had been wrong. Don't think about it, she whispered silently to herself.

Her eyes fastened on the mangled monstrosity that Baen had flown. It was some sort of contraption with a light metal frame and canvas wings. Apparently, it had flown all the way from Berth with Baen riding within. The thought was mind-boggling. Flying contraptions? It was almost absurd. Almost, but not quite, as she herself breathed poison, and her companions could do many unbelievable things as well. Once she considered that, flying metal didn't seem so strange. It was a shame he had destroyed it with his... interesting landing.

"Today we begin to search," Verre announced. "We'll break into teams of two, remaining within shouting distance of each other, and a half hour's walking distance. Cerise will search on her own, as she can cover more ground in wolf form." She hesitated. "Cerise, have you figured out what Pan meant about detecting magic? Because that would be useful right about now."

Everyone turned to Cerise. The now-familiar anger boiled up. She was a shape-shifter, so similar to the hybrid who had killed her mother. Too similar. A voice in the back of her head reminded her of one of her new-found memories.

You killed her, Blanca.

Taking a shuddering intake of breath, Blanca forced herself to focus on the conversation at hand. Thinking back to that day would only remind her that she really was a monster.

Cerise shook her head uncomfortably. "Sorry, I don't know what Pan meant. If I find out, I'll let you know."

"That's fine." Verre nodded. "Just let us know if anything changes. Is everyone clear on what we're doing? Only spend a few hours searching because we have no idea when the temperature will drop. We have a shelter, water, and now the meat that Cerise provided, so there's no need to rush. Any questions?"

Baen cleared his throat. "Can you please repeat that one more time, ma'am? I wasn't paying attention."

Verre rolled her eyes. "Does everyone else understand? I will be taking this fool with me, so it doesn't matter if he comprehends."

Everyone nodded except for Baen, who replied indignantly, "Fool? I'm not a fool! I flew all the way here in my own invention, thank you very much! I am utterly crushed to think that my beloved darling would treat me in such a cold manner."

"Get used to it," Aura chuckled. "That's how she treats all of us." Blanca almost laughed at that, her giggles hard to contain at Baen's furious face.

"Humor aside," Verre glared at Baen, "let's head out before we get caught up in your half-witted ways." She slung her pack over her shoulder and motioned for Baen to follow her.

"See you soon, my dear ladies." Baen grinned and winked before hurrying after Verre.

Blanca couldn't help the warm feeling that spread through her body. That was how a husband and wife should act, not screaming and crying, always afraid or angry. That was what Lyra deserved.

That's what your mother would have had too.

Ignoring the skin-crawling sound of Cerise morphing and her own agonizing thoughts, Blanca strode out of the cave, Aura having already left.

She didn't mind the quiet girl since Blanca hardly spoke herself. The chilly air tightened in her lungs, causing a quick shiver to run through her. The world was so blindingly white, even at such a low altitude of the mountain.

"It's so beautiful up here. Beautiful and different." Aura shouldered her satchel and grinned. "I always thought I'd love snow, but I didn't realize how much. Back where I'm from, it never snows. It's not even cold."

It seemed the quiet girl wasn't going to be nearly as quiet as she had hoped. Blanca sighed inwardly. As long as Aura did all the talking herself, she was fine.

It was still such an adjustment not being able to speak freely. She could only allow herself short, whispered sentences at most, and even then it always sent freezing fear rushing through her.

Making mistakes wasn't allowed. All it would take was one accident and Blanca could kill everyone. Her body tensed at the thought. How odd to be the one everyone feared instead of being the one in fear.

Time was passing far too fast for her to be able to to process her new changes—her body had simply adapted. Thinking about it, she realized that it had only been three weeks since she had first woken up to a green fog. It felt like she had been this weapon for an eternity.

"Blanca? Blanca, did you hear a word I said?" Aura rolled her eyes and flicked a handful of snow at her.

Blinking in surprise, Blanca realized she had zoned out. "Don't reply," Aura added quickly. "I know you didn't hear me, and I'd rather not experience poisonous breath, thanks. I asked which direction you think we should take?"

The words stung though Blanca knew Aura hadn't meant it to be rude. If she was in her place, she would most definitely not want a person who could breathe poison speaking to her. Still, it was obvious she was the outcast of the group and not by her own choice.

She shrugged in response to Aura, unsure of the direction to take. Or if Aura had actually even wanted her to reply. The mountainside all looked the same to her, drowned in brilliant white that was only broken by the dusty green of the trees. This entire quest of theirs had been stale, boring, and pointless. A pair of slippers? Why were they so important that Madame Rose would be willing to murder innocent people? It was like a child's game. An extremely dangerous child's game.

"Very well, I'll decide then. I say we head downward and west. It's more easily accessible, and I think the king is the type of person to depend more on magic than hard-to-reach places. Also, Pan mentioned that they would be easy to defend with whatever spells were on them. Anyone who might discover them would die."

The thought was far too ominous for Aura's cheery tone, but Blanca suspected she was just as worried as Blanca was. Magic was something her father had always hated, instilling a fear of it into her. Her stomach tied itself in knots at the thought of him. Even though her memory was still fragmented, he was a painfully real part of her story. She could imagine what he would do if he ever learned of her ability.

Though Madame Rose thought otherwise, this power wasn't a gift. It wasn't good; it was evil. It killed people with its deadly breath and brought horrific pain. All she wanted was to get rid of it and live happily with Lyra and Rose—was that so difficult?

Her long skirt caught in the deep snow, making it difficult to tromp through it. Blanca had been the only one to refuse the woolen trousers, preferring the skirts she was accustomed to.

Now she was beginning to regret having made that decision. Pulling on a long gown had always brought a smile to her face, and she would dance across the marble floors of her home as the skirt swished and sang. It became a tradition whenever she got a new gown. Her skirt did not swish now, and wet snow took the place of shining marble floors.

Aura trudged on ahead despite the fact that, though she was bundled heavily, her frame was still smaller than Blanca's.

The thought caused Blanca's already red cheeks to burn. The mirror had been right. She would never come close to being the fairest in the land.

Especially not to her father. Not after what she had done. Biting her lip so hard that it bled, she took a steadying breath and scolded herself. No more thoughts about her mother.

Blanca's mind turned back to Aura, and her fingers self-consciously grazed her cheek, feeling the plumpness of it. Was it too round? Aura and Verre had such lovely, pronounced cheekbones. Even Cerise, whose face was naturally round, had a thinner face than hers! Seeing their smaller bodies made her feel massive, especially since she stood over five and a half feet tall, taller than both Cerise and Aura.

Lyra had tried to combat her father's barbed words, but it wasn't the same. The painful truth was that Lord Rikor could say and do whatever he wanted, and Blanca would still love him. Unrequited love, yes, but love nonetheless.

"Do you know what to look for?" Aura called back without stopping. "Because I know very little about magic. I would think that you, a nobleman's daughter, would know, though. So, have any ideas?"

Blanca chuckled, glad for the distance between them as poison spilled out. How wrong Aura was. If only she knew what her father had been like, what a monster he had been. She gave a little shrug, and Aura turned to trudge onward.

Her memories were still slowly returning, little thoughts and sights triggering them. But there were no more flashbacks. She often wondered why they had stopped, not that she minded.

But it was also only those flashback memories that she kept reliving, the pain and terror always fresh. They haunted her thoughts and dreams, reminding her how broken she was. For some reason, the pain was important to who she was. But there was one memory she couldn't remember no matter how hard she tried. It haunted her with its ghost of a presence, tortured her with half-thoughts.

She could not remember how she died.

AURA

TRAVELING HAD ALWAYS been something Aura had dreamed about. She would close her eyes and pretend that she was somewhere other than the filthy shack where she lived, imagining that she was somewhere in a large, quiet forest, cool breezes gently bringing the scent of flowers.

And snow.

She envisioned herself surrounded by snowflakes, each falling softly down, some nestling in her dark hair. It was the image she always brought to mind when she needed to calm herself. She had not pictured a howling storm, each flake like a miniature dagger, stinging her raw skin.

The Bluefrost Mountains seemed set on destroying her vision of what snow was like. Her fingers and toes were solid ice, dragging through the endless sea of white. Blanca was faring far better than her, despite the fact that she was wearing a ridiculous floor-length dress.

She was a strange girl. Aura didn't know what to make of her. There was something that seemed to be affecting her deeply, causing her to flinch at loud noises or just zone out, unblinking.

She was the most secretive of all of them, not even explaining who Lyra and Rose were. Aura wondered if her father had died and that was the reason she was so quiet. That and the fact that her breath was poison.

"Isn't it so beautiful?" Blanca breathed, her eyes shining. "I've always loved snow, but this is breathtaking!" The wind was blowing so fiercely that it ripped her poison away from them, spiraling it into the distance.

"Blanca! Do you even see where we are? My feet are frozen, I feel like my nose is gone, and I'm starving! There is nothing beautiful about any of this."

Aura glared at Blanca, wondering if the crazy girl even realized they were stuck in a blizzard, their bodies almost frozen solid. Breathtaking was not the word she would have used, not even close.

Sure, if she were to consider it, there was a certain wild and primitive beauty to the storm, but she was too frozen to remain fixed on the thought.

"Where I'm from, it snows often, so I'm used to blizzards such as this." Blanca watched as the green mist disappeared quickly, her eyes brightening. "You're from Oobay, though, right? I've never visited it, but I've heard of the sweltering heat. This must be quite a change for you."

What was quite the change was hearing Blanca speak more than one sentence. It also surprised her that Blanca even remembered where she was from. Perhaps she had paid more attention than Aura had originally given her credit for.

"Yes, it is an adjustment. In Oobay, people do anything possible to avoid the heat. During the dry season, many people die from lack of water and sunstroke.

"It's a nightmare, sweat pouring from everyone's bodies; children whimpering at the street corners; people driven insane by the sun." Despite the vividness of the memories, it was hard to even picture that terrible heat in such intense cold.

"I can't even begin to imagine what that must have been like. It makes me shudder just to think about it." Blanca glanced back at her with almost pity in her eyes. The look turned to worry quickly as she continued, "Do you know how to get back? I can't tell what time it is, and we haven't found anything yet. I think it would be best to go back to the cave."

Aura froze, this time with fear. Could they make it back? With the blinding white storm that had caught them unawares, it was hard to even make out the trees just a few yards in front of her. "What direction is the cave? I know we headed west, but I don't think we're still headed that way." She swallowed, fighting the panic that rose to overwhelm her. "I think we're lost."

They were going to die. Aura could no longer feel her toes, and she imagined what it would be like for her whole body to become like that: numb and unresponsive. To drown beneath the snow, her body becoming like a solid rock...

A blood-curdling shriek echoed through the wall of white that seemed to surround them. Heart hammering, Aura whirled all around, trying to decipher where the sound had come from. Another shriek followed, sending shivers coursing down her spine.

"Aura," Blanca whispered, huddling close, "what was that?"

She had absolutely no idea, but whatever it was, it was angry. Her limbs grew weak as the shriek continued, climbing in pitch and volume.

"Blanca, we need to run very fast very soon—otherwise there is a good chance we will die an extremely painful death." She grasped her hand and ran, not caring which direction they went.

Her legs felt like boards, and her feet caught in the deep snow, throwing her to the ground. She scrambled back up, only for searing pain to shoot up her leg. Whimpering, she collapsed again.

"Aura! We have to keep moving!" Blanca froze when she saw Aura's expression. "Oh, no! What happened?" She knelt down beside her to inspect her leg. "I can't tell much with your pant leg in the way, but it seems to be swelling."

Aura blinked back tears as she clutched her ankle. She had sprained ankles before, but this was bad, very bad. Why did she have such horrible luck? The pain was hot, licking away at the numbness of her leg. If she hadn't been so frozen, the pain would probably have been worse. While death by mysterious beast wasn't how she expected to die, it was still rather heroic. Perhaps they would write a story about her.

A deep growl reverberated around her. Aura clenched her jaw and turned to Blanca. "Keep running. Hopefully my death will slow the dragon, beast—whatever it is—long enough for you to escape."

"Dragon!" squeaked Blanca. "There's a dragon?" Another deafening roar caused Blanca to bolt upright. "I'm sorry, Aura. If I die... Well, I can't stay." She gave one last regretful look before gathering up her skirt and running.

Aura sat stunned for a few seconds. She had actually run away? Well, at least she would be safe, but still... "Coward," she muttered as she eased herself upright, tensing as pain engulfed her body. She hadn't said she was sure. It could have been some other carnivorous beast set on devouring them. If it happened to be a dragon, though, did they have a good sense of smell? Because that would be a terrible misfortune.

Through the blinding white came a grey shadow. A gigantic grey shadow with wings and shining black eyes.

The dragon's long black talons dug deep into the snow, its large feet resting easily without sinking. Its long, lithe body was shimmering white, and its beautiful, pristine wings draped regally over its shoulders. If Aura hadn't been about to die a gruesome death, she might have squealed with joy.

Sniffing carefully, its eyes alighted on Aura. "Who dares enter my mountainside without my authority?" Its voice was thunderous and yet graceful. Aura stared in amazement that such a creature would even speak to her.

"You're absolutely breathtaking."

The dragon seemed startled, drawing back slightly as its wings fluttered. "Are you speaking to me, Cevata, Ancient One of Ice, Wind, and Snow, Guardian of the Bluefrost Mountains?"

Aura's eyes widened. She bowed hastily, wincing as she did so. "My gracious and wise Cevata, I did not know this was your domain, otherwise I would not have set foot without your express permission.

And I simply was commenting on the magnificence of your beauty, oh lovely Cevata." Aura's eyes darted back up at the dragon, her hands clasped together in a vain attempt to stop trembling. She hadn't expected dragons to have such long teeth. Or talons. Or wings.

The dragon pulled back slightly, head tilting. "Such reverence from your kind is unusual. In fact, you're the first to approach me as something other than a monster to be slain." Her tongue ran over her large, sharp teeth, causing a wave of terror to wash over Aura. "Why are you here?"

Gulping nervously and hoping that maybe she wouldn't be eaten, Aura gave a weak smile. "My friend and I were exploring the mountainside. The storm made us lose our sense of direction. We're only trying to get back to our camp." She struggled to stay upright, the cold and pain becoming too much to handle. "She and I got separated when you arrived."

"You're injured." Cevata blinked slowly, her obsidian eyes contrasting the paleness of her scales as she studied them. "I doubt you'll be able to make it back to your camp like this. For your respect, I will allow you and your friend to ride on my back to return to your camp. This is an honor that must not be taken lightly. Is that understood?"

Aura nodded furiously, relief bringing a cautious smile to her face. Her heart dropped as Cevata gently deposited her on her smooth silverish-white scales. As she was lifted up, Aura saw them.

There were the slippers, hanging from a black chain around Cevata's neck. They were a beautiful, pulsing red, but her view was cut short as she settled onto Cevata's back.

All thoughts fled her brain, her heart thudding loudly in her chest.

What in all of Denthlire...? But the more Aura considered it, the more it made sense. What better way to protect them? But she couldn't say anything yet. Who knew what Cevata might do?

The dragon lifted off, Aura's stomach dropping as they rose swiftly. The cold air stung at Aura's already raw face, but the storm had disappeared. Upon further inspection, however, Aura discovered that the storm hadn't stopped but merely swirled around Cevata; she was the eye of the storm.

The ground sped by below, Aura almost missing Blanca's tiny figure running through the snow. "There! She's right there." Cevata began a graceful descent, landing just in front of a terror-stricken Blanca. They descended so rapidly that Aura scraped her knuckles against the rough ridges of Cevata's back.

"Blanca, it's alright. The Ancient One, Cevata, has agreed to help us back to the cave instead of eating us," Aura said, grinning.

Blanca frowned and took a tentative step back. "How do I know this is not some trick that the dragon has placed on me? What if I'm simply going to be eaten later?"

Cevata chuckled, fog issuing from her throat. "You both have the wrong idea of what it is that I do. I am the Guardian of the Bluefrost Mountains. I only kill, and I never eat those who venture into the areas they're not allowed to be. Human flesh is not as delicious as you might think."

A theory began to form in Aura's head, but she refrained from saying anything; she would discuss it later. Blanca remained unmoved, her expression fearful.

Aura didn't have the time to reason with her, knowing that Cevata could change her mind at any moment. She allowed herself to slip into Blanca's mind, nearly pulling back when she sensed the overwhelming fear that resided in her. It was constant fear, not just from the dragon. A fear that had been instilled in her and had never left. Usually, Aura had to probe for emotions, but not so with Blanca. There was also hatred, boiling hatred that began to eat away at Aura's control. Her concentration slipped, and panic set in. The anger was palpable, and Aura began to feel fury rise up inside of herself too. Sleep, she commanded hurriedly, Blanca slumping to the ground almost instantly. Aura withdrew from her mind with a sigh of relief.

"My," Cevata commented in surprise, "what a unique gift that is. Quite powerful, too. You would do well to use it wisely." Brows furrowed in confusion, Aura nodded. How Cevata even knew that was beyond her, but she wasn't risking incurring the dragon's wrath.

Cevata lifted Blanca up in front of Aura, who held her tightly. "She's a peculiar girl, this one; I could tell that from even just the brief time I spent in her mind. Beware, there is a darkness to her I am not fond of."

The ominous tone of Cevata's rumbling voice made a cold chill seep into Aura. She had glimpsed that same hate and fear, and it had nearly made her lose control. Whatever had brought such pain and suffering— so that it would infect Blanca's very mind—must be terrifying indeed. Cevata was right; she would have to be wary.

21

CERISE

THERE WAS SUCH a thrill in treading lightly over the snow without stumbling or being frozen. Cerise yipped happily as she bounded over a mound of snow, her nose taking in numerous scents at once. This was the longest she had ever remained in wolf form, and it was exhilarating. Her body was stronger, her senses sharper, and she was actually enjoying it.

But it also brought back memories of Raina.

Raina. The name brought fear gnawing at her flesh every time. It also brought memories of how the woman would hit her until it made her shift in rage, or how she would force her to hunt, all the while wearing a magical collar that wouldn't let her shift or run away.

She had been a powerful witch, one who all the villagers would turn to when in need. She would manipulate them, cursing whole families with sores only she could heal and then charging them extravagant prices to remove them. The lord of the town had been a push-over, preferring to drown his worries in alcohol and lavish parties, so Raina had near-complete control of Lithrium.

Cerise and her father had moved there once her mother had left to lead her pack. Her father saw what Raina was doing to the people and tried to stop it.

Cerise had been only eleven when Raina had murdered him, driving an enchanted dagger through his ribcage, killing him before he even hit the ground.

Cerise remembered feeling like her heart had been ripped to shreds. That was the first time she had shifted, a snarling pup trying to kill a seasoned witch.

The memory of the pain had disappeared, but her mind... that was what she remembered. It was like her consciousness was being ripped away from her body, placed in the corner of her mind where she could merely watch.

She had never been afraid of herself, but that overwhelming bloodlust, the fact that she had ripped out Raina's throat and felt no remorse—that was what haunted her even now.

Of course, just a child, she had tried to attack and had been grabbed and enslaved from that day on. Only seven years later had she been strong enough to finally kill her.

A magical pull came upon her, so strong she stumbled. Shaking snow from her fur, she whirled around, bewildered.

The pull came again, an irresistible force. Forest breezes... warm, crackling fires... It was potent and beautiful magic, something she had to discover. Maybe she should just leave the group and run until her legs gave out and she became drunk on the taste of freedom.

Spell of enticing.

Cerise backed up quickly, more alarmed by the fact that she had recognized the spell than by the fact that she could have just died. She had never been able to recognize spells before when Raina had used them. Why now?

Shaking her head, Cerise moved tentatively to the left, hackles raised.

A wall of flames rose up before her, crackling with such intense heat that it singed her fur.

Spell of burning.

Limbs trembling, Cerise backed away and headed toward the cave. Just because she could sense them didn't mean she needed to experience them.

And while the spells were terrifying, it meant she was on the right track. She would have to bring the others back tomorrow, but that meant telling them about her ability.

Prejudice was something Cerise was all too familiar with. It was less obvious as a child, but now she knew that her parents had made sure she didn't hear the hateful comments.

Since her father was a mage, no one had tried anything, but all the children would avoid her, leaving her to play with only herself and her parents. It had been confusing when her parents had told her gravely that she could walk with Mama or Papa but never with both.

It had only been much later when she carried out errands for Raina that she realized how much people hated hybrids. Just because they were different.

She was actually starting to like some of the other young women, but sharing about her new abilities would make them hate her.

The thought caused an ache to build in her chest, and for a second her eyes burned with unshed tears. Verre, despite her cold exterior, was actually quite caring though she tried to hide it. She seemed to be the only one who truly didn't care that she was a werewolf. Well, Aura might not care either, but Blanca definitely hated Cerise. She seemed to hold a grudge against werewolves for some reason that she wouldn't discuss. Cerise doubted that hatred would disappear once Blanca found out she was a hybrid.

Running lightly over the snow, Cerise allowed herself to relax as the cold air ruffled her brown fur. She was used to the balmy weather of Lithrium, but the blustery, cold weather of the mountains was lovely. Perhaps her mother had journeyed here with her pack, each member barking happily as they waded through the deep snow. The thought made Cerise homesick for a life she had never known.

As she ran, she remained alert for Pan. He had said to call him when they had accomplished what they had come to do, but she doubted he would leave them unsupervised.

Upon nearing the cave, a strange and powerful smell assaulted her. It made her want to cower and surrender to whatever it was.

Shaking the embarrassing thought away, Cerise skulked towards the cave, her body tense for any potential attack. There was also a strong magical atmosphere, but she could not read it like she had been able to before. All she knew was that it was ancient—ancient and powerful.

The snow fluttered. Cerise growled deep in her throat, her body slung low. A ripple moved across a massive patch of snow, and with a whimper of fear, she realized it was not snow at all. Wise, black eyes blinked slowly at her, cold air brushing against her. "Hello, small wolf. I would ask what you're doing so far from your pack, but I believe they're right here."

Aura scrambled down from the dragon's back. "Cerise! You're here. Verre and Baen have yet to return. This is Cevata, Ancient One of Ice, Wind, and Snow, Guardian of the Bluefrost Mountains."

So that was the magic she had detected. Cevata's magic was almost overwhelming, so abundant, so intricate, that Cerise couldn't decipher the individual aspects. The dragon was a sparkling white, its talons and eyes contrasting with deepest black.

"Hmm," Cevata rumbled, "what unique magic you possess, and so much of it locked away. Perhaps I can help you fix that."

A chill set in Cerise's bones. Well, at least she didn't have to tell them now... right?

Cevata shifted slightly, toppling several trees. She was massive, probably near the size of the palace itself. "Did you know werewolves were among the first creatures to be created? Lune, the Ancient One of Light, created them so that they would praise his moonlight. Powerful creatures they are, though that power has been diluted over time."

It was astonishing to think that Cevata had been around since the beginning of time, to consider all the wars, love, and monarchies she had seen grow and die. All the lives that had passed in the blink of an eye and the power she had seen beings possess.

"I never knew that about werewolves," Aura said in awe. "What an amazing ancestry!" She started to walk toward Cerise but fell with a cry of pain.

"Ah, yes. Your injury." Cevata bent her head down and breathed over the ankle. Swirling ice crystals appeared, settling over her ankle and vanishing. The pained look on Aura's face disappeared as she rotated it slowly.

"Thank you." Aura bowed reverently.

"You're by far one of the most interesting bands of humans I've met. I will allow you free passage through this area of the mountains, but know that I might not be so gracious should you decide to venture west once more." Cevata rose, her great wings unfurling. "And Cerise, should you need help with your magic, I would be more than willing to share some of my wisdom. A gift like yours is rare and must be cultivated properly."

If Cerise had held onto to any hope that they didn't realize what Cevata was speaking of, that was now gone. She swallowed nervously and nodded.

Cevata narrowed her eyes, her gaze flickering for a second upon Blanca. "Yes, should you have need of me, simply speak my name. I shall answer."

With one powerful sweep of her wings, she lifted elegantly from the ground, creating a wind storm below. In just a second, she was gone, leaving behind a small flurry of snow.

Blanca turned to Cerise, her eyes cold, but she said nothing, simply stared and left for the cave.

"I have something I must share with you all," Aura stated excitedly, her face bright red from the cold. "I may have discovered where the slippers are!"

Cerise ignored her, allowing her body to shift to human form. A quick examination showed that again her clothing had shifted with her. Shivering from the sudden exposure to the cold, she answered, "I have something to share too. We should all wait in the cave until Verre returns and then share what we found; it's nearly evening anyway. It may not take as long to retrieve the slippers as we had first thought."

Aura nodded. "I think we might actually survive this. Do you think we should update Pan on our findings? Or do you think he already knows?"

The thought was a disturbing one though she had wondered the same thing herself. Cerise vowed to do her very best to succeed. Otherwise Pan would not hesitate to slaughter her mother and entire pack. Any mistake, no matter how small, would not be tolerated. "I'm sure he knows everything he needs to. Should he want to know more, he will contact us."

Cerise stretched slowly as she walked to the cave, her muscles sore. She had traveled miles while searching, and only now was she feeling the effects of such a strenuous task.

All she wanted to do was curl up and sleep, but that was not allowed, especially since she needed to explain about her new abilities. Abilities she herself didn't even fully understand. And considering what Cevata had said... could there be more?

Her father had been able to manipulate all the elements but only to a certain extent. Still, she had always thought it fascinating when he would make a small flower turn into a huge bush. Perhaps her powers were the same.

Settling to the ground in the cave, she rifled through her pack, finding a dried piece of meat. She tore at it ravenously, her body craving nutrients. Aura and Blanca followed close after her, each grabbing food as well. The cold weather had starved them all, and the fresh water in their water skins was especially satisfying.

Cerise let the cool drink trickle down her throat, savoring every drop. It would be foolish to guzzle it, as it could make her sick, and then it would be a waste.

Cerise curled up on her cloak, just starting to get drowsy. It had been an exhausting day, and her body pled for rest. Verre didn't come while Cerise watched the fire begin to dim. Had she gotten lost? Had she been killed by a spell?

The last one troubled her especially. If it weren't for this new-found power, she'd be dead herself. Verre and Baen didn't have that advantage, and they couldn't afford to lose Verre.

This new power of hers helped, but she didn't understand it, and it didn't guarantee that she wouldn't die. If only she could talk to her parents for even just a moment. They'd be able to help.

As she reminisced about her mother's fierce hugs and her father's warm eyes, Cerise remembered something. Something that shocked her to her core.

"Werewolves come of age at eighteen, sweetheart. Maybe that's when your magic will appear." Her mother's loving gaze was hazy in her memory, and Cerise couldn't remember what it felt like to have her arms around her. But those words her mother had said all those years ago remained stuck in her head now, replaying over and over.

She was coming into her full powers.

22

VERRE

VERRE STILL COULDN'T believe that Baen was here with her. She almost wanted to run a shard of glass across her palm to check if she was dreaming, but that would affect her throwing accuracy, and she couldn't afford to be injured.

Glancing over at Baen walking beside her, she grinned again. A silly, happy grin that made her feel like a fool.

"What's on your mind?" he teased, elbowing her affectionately. "Thinking of how much you desperately love me?"

It was true, even though normally she would never admit it. Things had changed, though. She now realized how short life really was and how easy it was to lose everything.

"Yes, I am thinking about how much I love you. Baen, I love you more than life, my abilities as a fighter, more than my parents, or anything else in this world. You're my jester, and I'll always be your ice princess."

Next thing she knew, Baen was kissing her. His hands held her waist firmly as he pressed her up against a tree, stopping any other words she could have said.

And Verre didn't care. She didn't care about the mission, the fact that they were in serious danger... none of it. All she cared about was that Baen was here, his arms wrapped around her, enveloping her in their reassuring warmth; the simple act said so much more than words ever could.

All she could think about was his lips on hers in a desperate sort of kiss, as if to make up for all the time lost. Her hands tangled in his hair, pulling him impossibly closer.

She broke away, already regretting doing so.

"We have a mission to complete. I'd love to continue but—"

He nodded, his eyes twinkling. "Of course, the mission. But I'm not letting you forget that you confessed your love for all the world to hear."

She laughed, kissed him once more, and pushed him away. "Come along, Jester, we don't have time for spontaneous kisses." Oh, how she wanted to grab him once more and resume from where they had left off, but she couldn't let emotion dictate her actions, not when Baen's life was on the line.

"What a pity, beloved," Baen remarked, playful sadness evident on his features. "Spontaneous kisses are among the best."

It was so good to have his cheery annoyance back. Perhaps everything would work out after all. "Did you bring anything with you that could help us detect magic? According to Pan, there are all sorts of dangerous spells planted along this mountainside."

"Spells? Magic? Dangerous! Darling, I was trying to be heroic and noble by coming to find you, but I did not expect to die from an unknown spell. Unfortunately, this does put a damper on our relationship." He sighed heavily, making a light tsking sound. "Also, no, I did not come prepared to deal with magic. A warning might have been nice. Also, who is this Pan fellow? Should I be concerned?" Baen glanced over at her and winked.

It appeared nothing had changed between them, for which Verre was glad. Rolling her eyes, she socked him on the shoulder. "My dear man, if a simple spell should deter you from pursuing a woman, perhaps you shouldn't pursue her at all. And Pan has threatened to kill us all, so yes, you should be worried."

With a repentant look, he snaked his arm around her waist as they walked. "Ice Princess, I would pursue you to the ends of Atulau should it mean that I get to spend every moment of life with you."

"Cut the flowery words short; you know I prefer simple language." She teasingly pushed him away and strode on ahead. "We're looking for an extremely powerful and dangerous object which is most likely hidden deep within the heart of the mountains. This should be easy, right?"

Now that Baen was here with her, it made it all the more dire that she execute this flawlessly. The task seemed impossible, and there was a good chance it was, but there was no way for her to back out. So it was time to clear her mind and look at it from a sensible manner, no emotions attached.

If she were to hide something in the mountainside, where would she? And how?

Hiding the slippers in the heart of the mountain seemed like it would have been a good idea since only a massive explosion or a mage could uncover it. Add some powerful spells, and no one would find it. It was the obvious choice, which meant it was the wrong one. The king was fond of his little games, games that often injured his own people. Like the dragon hunt he had invented a decade ago, where he forced twenty young adults to search for and slay a dragon in exchange for their lives.

None had returned. The thought still made her stomach churn.

Verre paused walking to look around her. Yes, the king was a twisted and cruel man, so it would make sense that he would apply that same evil to hiding his most coveted possession. It was likely he had employed brutal methods of keeping people away from the slippers.

Though, Verre wasn't even certain he had been the one to hide them. The slippers had been lost—hidden—for centuries. Any one of the rulers in that time could have hidden them. It made sense, though, for King Jore to have re-hidden them, afraid of them being found.

One thing about it all that still bothered Verre was the fact that the slippers were meant only for the feet of Dorthea. Anyone else who tried to wield the magic died. So why did Madame Rose want them? Realization dawned on Verre, her pulse quickening. Unless they were never Dorthea's to begin with...

What if Dorthea had only stolen them from an even more powerful magic-wielder?

If this theory proved true, then Madame Rose could wreak havoc on all of Atulau. She would be unstoppable.

What if Verre refused to retrieve the slippers? The question wormed its way through her defenses, but she pushed it away almost instantly.

No.

That meant death for Baen and her parents. She could not be the reason they died; she couldn't bear to lose them. She would give Madame Rose what she wanted and then flee. She would take Baen and her parents and get as far away from Allegora as possible. They could hide in some small Evanscenian seaport for the rest of their days for all she cared. She refused to let Madame Rose take away the only thing that mattered to her.

"Verre? You've been slowly veering from the direction you said we should go." Baen chuckled at his own joke, but Verre's face remained neutral. Glancing around, she readjusted, making sure to follow east on her compass.

"No laugh? Not even a smile?" Baen sobered instantly, as if realizing that Verre was focusing on her task. "Okay, what should we be looking for?"

That was one of the things that had drawn Verre to Baen. Even though he loved to tease and jest, he could also be serious if he had to. He knew when she wasn't in the mood for merriment.

"Anything magical. That's the best I can say. We were given very little information, unfortunately. Be careful, though. Magic is tricky business, and you never know what you could be dealing with."

A chilling howl cut off any response Baen could have made. *Cerise?* Two more followed in haunting harmony, and any hope that it was her was dashed. Besides, the howls were not canine; they were far more strange, a tortured edge to each note. There was also a hunger to it that brought goosebumps to Verre's arms.

"Please tell me I was the only one who heard that," Baen whispered, eyes darting about.

Verre sighed, long glass shards appearing in each hand. "Regretfully, no. Here, take a shard. I'd like to say that those sounds were from nothing dangerous, but that will most likely prove false."

Baen gulped and grabbed the glass, handling it gingerly.

The howls grew more frenzied, the pitch rising so that it rang in her ears. Whatever the creatures were, they were surrounding them, Verre picking out swiftly moving blurs.

Allowing her mind to narrow to one thought, Verre created a glass spear, every detail perfect down to the razor-sharp point.

It was time to kill.

The first blur erupted from the treeline, crazed eyes and a drooling maw all Verre saw before she drove the spear through its skull.

The thing whimpered once, rolling to a halt as Verre removed her spear in time to bat away the next. There were five that she could see, one already dead. Baen was wrestling his shard away from another one of them.

She clenched her fists and concentrated, sending a dozen shards into the two creatures who were headed straight for Baen.

Stabbing the fourth through the ribcage, Verre was finally able to see what they were dealing with. As soon as she did, she regretted it with every fiber of her being.

They were women. Some young, some wrinkled with age, but all definitely female. Though it seemed they had ceased to be human long ago.

Greenish-grey scales covered them, and odd-fitting jaws bulged from their mouths, complete with jagged and dripping fangs. Their limbs were long and crooked, as if their bones had grown too quickly for their bodies.

It was sickening, especially since Verre knew who they were. They were the handmaidens the king turned into engineered killers with his disgusting trigor experiments.

Whirling her spear around, she faced the last one, Baen having dispatched his. The creature shuffled awkwardly, drool and poison dripping from its jaws. It hissed and snapped, but did not attack, eyeing Verre's spear carefully. It cut at Verre's heart to have to kill the creature, knowing that there was someone in Allegora who was wishing that their daughter, sister, or wife would come home.

The thought distracted Verre, and the creature lunged, narrowly missing her shoulder with its long claws. Sympathy gone, she shot a volley of shards from her body, catching her breath as the creature fell with a howl, sludge-like brown blood seeping into the snow around it.

Far-away howls echoed through the woods, as if mourning the loss of the dead creatures at Verre's feet. She rushed to Baen, wrapping him in a tight hug. "Are you injured? Their claws and fangs are probably poisoned. We need to leave before more come." She babbled on, visibly shaking. Usually she was alone for this part, when all her emotions came ripping out of her like a raging storm she couldn't control.

Then the horrible guilt set in.

Who killed others? What kind of monster did that make her? She was always disgusted with herself despite the fact that it'd been necessary. Had it been right to kill those women who had been forced into the experiments? Verre could only hope she had finally given them peace.

Baen said nothing as she shook, just stroked her hair, whispering words of love and encouragement. Eventually, the shaking stopped. She pulled away, wiping her eyes hastily. "We need to go. It's starting to get late, and we should warn the others of the creatures."

He nodded. "Yes, it would be wise to head back. I'm starving, and I'm sure you're hungry too. Plus, you're freezing. Some food and warmth would help tremendously."

"They were the women the king forced into his trigor experiments," she said abruptly. "My father was asked to contribute, but he refused. They were his concubines, Baen. They had no choice, and look what happened to them." Unable to continue, Verre walked briskly through the snow beside him, locking her emotions in and burying them deep. This was also part of the process.

Once she regained control, she refused to act on the pain and guilt any longer, hiding it away deep inside.

"I... I'm sorry. I've always known about what you do, but I never..." Baen turned to face her, voice rough with pain. "Just know that I love you and I always will. Despite the monsters you face and the guilt you feel. You will forever be the home of my heart." He moved to embrace her, but froze, his eyes fastening on something above her.

Overwhelming fear flooded Verre as she glanced up. There, flying above, was the largest dragon she had ever seen. Granted, it was also the first, but it was at least the size of her parent's manor, which was large even by Berth standards. The dragon paid no attention to them but kept flying on, soon disappearing into the clouds.

It had come from the direction of the cave.

Verre ran as she never had before, her long legs quickly covering ground. Coming to a sudden stop at the mouth of the cave and seeing the three safe, she exploded, "What is going on? Why in the world did I just see a big, blazing dragon!"

Cerise sighed. "You might want to sit down. It's a long story."

23
BLANCA

BLANCA SAT QUIETLY as Cerise explained what had happened to the three of them. Judging by the awful stench that rose from the ooze splattered on Verre's clothing, she had an interesting tale as well.

As Cerise spoke of the dragon, Blanca glowered. She had no recollection of riding the dragon—up until the very end, of course—only of blacking out after she had refused to climb on. Aura hadn't said anything, but Blanca guessed she was the reason for her sudden lapse of memory.

"Blanca, could I have a word in private?" Verre's serious tone sent chills up Blanca's spine. Whatever they were going to discuss, it couldn't be good.

She gave the assassin a quick nod and followed her out into the cold.

"I want you to kill Pan," Verre stated bluntly. "He's clearly afraid of your poison, and I think he's vulnerable to it. When we find the slippers and give them to him, I want you to make sure he never makes it back to Denthlire. Don't mention this to anyone else, understood?"

Verre wanted her to be her assassin. Her. Blanca. Her limbs began to shake and it wasn't from the cold. Madame Rose's command came to mind.

Kill them.

She couldn't do it, but would Verre be suspicious if she refused? It was the right decision to choose Madame Rose.

Right?

Right.

Swallowing nervously, she met Verre's steely grey eyes. "Understood."

Glancing around, Blanca realized that far too soon they would all be dead.

Because of her.

She wasn't a killer, but maybe she could be. Her father hadn't minded hurting people—he had taken pleasure in it. That cruelty tainted her own blood. If she didn't think about what she would have to do, then maybe she could tap into that anger that lived inside her. Maybe she could be a monster.

Like a fractured dam, the guilt came roaring back, so strong that she could barely take a single breath.

She had killed her mother just like she was going to kill all of them.

Blanca was more like her father than she realized. They had both caused pain on their family. They both were broken. They were both monsters.

But this time, she was doing this for Lyra and Rose, she told herself. If she didn't kill them, her family would be killed. One enraged scream could dispatch them all. In fact, as she glanced around, she could destroy them all at that very moment. The cave closed them in enough for it, but she resisted, knowing that she wouldn't be able to find the slippers on her own. That, and the fact that thinking about it and actually doing it were two vastly different things.

"So, Aura tried to charm a dragon? That's ridiculously stupid, but I guess it worked." Verre rolled her eyes, as if she was used to these sorts of things. She probably was.

Verre was the most frightening of the group, though Blanca was now wary of Aura. Everyone but Blanca had some sort of skill besides their magical abilities. Verre was a natural fighter, Aura knew how to survive, and Cerise was a mixture of both. All Blanca could do was read, write, and recite Allegorian history to perfection. She could also bake amazing crescentberry rolls.

"Yes, it was insane, I will admit, but what happened to you? Get into a fight with Baen?" Chuckles reverberated through the room, the loudest being Baen himself. Verre frowned at the lot of them, their laughter dying instantly.

Blanca gulped as Verre's penetrating grey eyes locked onto her own. It felt like she was boring deep into Blanca's soul and mind, uncovering all of her secrets.

"Some odd creatures attacked us. There were five of them, as if they were a pack."

Blanca noticed Cerise perk up at the mention of pack and remembered that her mother was a werewolf. Werewolves were frightening beings. Every child knew of the haunting lullaby their mothers would sing:

Watch your toes as you climb into bed
People with wolf skins would like you dead
Listen for howls on cold winter nights
And pay heed to those with teeth that bite

Shuddering, Blanca returned her attention to Verre, unable to completely shake the chill that had set in her bones.

"Have you ever heard the tale of the trigor experiments?" Verre asked. "How the king tortured his handmaids, injecting them with trigor poisoning? I think those were the women, or used to be, anyway."

The trigor experiments—Blanca remembered hearing about them. Her father had laughed and stated that the women had no doubt deserved it and downed another glass of wine.

From Verre's tone, they must have morphed into something horrible. How could the king have done such a thing? Those women had stood no chance, none at all. He was supposed to be their protector. Their king. Not a monster.

"Anyway," Verre added quickly, sensing the somber mood, "Baen, you never actually gave us the details of how you got here. Perhaps you could tell the tale?"

Blanca was relieved at the change of subject; it seemed they all were. Allegora was a mess politically, and no one liked discussing it.

"Yes, that's right. You know nothing of my daring attempt at a rescue." Baen sat up, his eyes twinkling. "It started when I went to check in on Verre since that's just the great sort of husband I am." He ducked a blow from Verre before continuing. "I knew something was wrong when I noticed that furniture was upturned and the room was messy, especially with broken glass.

"Verre is a perfectionist and always has to have things a certain way. Spying no blood, I realized that she was not dead, but most likely in danger. But besides my clever deductions, I was lost."

He held up a finger. "But I had an idea. There was an old witch who lived not far from the manor. She had limited foretelling abilities, and could often see people or things that were in other parts of Atulau. If anyone could help me find Verre, it was her.

"I quickly ran to her small cottage, upsetting a few of her rather nasty cats. It appeared she had known I would come and was not entirely happy to see me. I poured on my good charm, even washing her disgusting dishes, which seemed to have served as a hairball holder.

"Upon seeing what a good and noble man I was, she agreed to search for you for me. For a price, of course."

At this point Verre rolled her eyes but affectionately nudged Baen. "Good? Noble? Charming? I wouldn't call you any of those."

Blanca couldn't help but grin as Baen gave Verre a kiss on her nose. "I'm sure you'd call me far greater things, like beyond virtuous and an absolutely wonderful husband. But as I was saying, the witch succumbed to my wit and charm easily and offered to share the information at a reasonable price. She brought me into this dark room where she invoked a spell, and suddenly the room was a forest. I quickly realized that I was simply being shown an immersive image. After a few failed attempts, I finally saw you, Verre, in a castle. I nearly went to go search through all the castles, but then the witch—whose name was Ramona, I believe—bluntly told me that you were in Denthlire and that there was no way to get there, not unless I wanted to certainly die trying.

"She must have taken pity on me, for she let me come every day after that to watch you. For days this happened." Baen's voice caught, and he quickly cleared his throat. "I started to build a machine that could allow me to fly because I was determined that I would go and find you. Then one day, you weren't in the castle, but in the mountains, surrounded by snow. Ramona told me they were the Bluefrost Mountains, gave me the exact directions based on the stars, and sent me on my way, relieved to be rid of me. My metalwing worked beautifully, and I reached the mountains in a fraction of the time it would have taken on foot. And here I am," he finished, an arm around Verre.

A metalwing. Blanca had seen the contraption and couldn't believe it had flown Baen—a decent-sized man—up a mountain! It was a different kind of magic, the workings of oil and gears. The magic that made metal fly and wheels turn of their own accord.

For a moment, Blanca wished she had that kind of magic, the magic of hard work and dirty hands, instead of the magic of poison, of death.

214

"What an adventure," Aura said, starry-eyed, legs crossed and eating a haunch of hark. "Did you really build the metalwing?"

Baen nodded, eyes twinkling. "I did indeed! Denthlire isn't accessible on foot, so I was hoping—before Verre left there, of course—that I could fly there. I don't have any magic or special abilities that would enable me to go to Denthlire, unlike your friend Pan. So I used the talent I do have: inventing.

"It took quite a few trial and error attempts but nothing I couldn't handle. I'm proud to say that the metalwing is airworthy. Er, was airworthy."

It was an impressive feat. Blanca glanced outside where the crushed metal contraption rested. A grin made its way onto her face as she remembered his awkward crash. Any hope of him having a dramatic entrance had also been crushed when he fell so gracefully into the snow below.

Still, Blanca wondered what it would be like to fly it. To feel the earth fall away beneath her, to have the cold air take away her breath, and to feel her hair flowing in the wind. She would be far away from everything, having only herself and the expansive sky.

Cerise, who had been unusually quiet, finally spoke. "I have something to share with you all."

Everyone turned to her, their eyes questioning. Blanca tensed, her heart pounding. Whatever Cerise was going to share, she didn't want to hear it. Werewolves had never done the world any good.

"I have discovered that power Pan told us about. The dragon, Cevata, also confirmed it. When near mage magic, I can detect and decipher it. It's like looking at a book and knowing exactly what it's about. When I'm near a spell, I can understand what the spell does and how dangerous it is. Today I encountered two, and both were brutally terrifying." Cerise shuddered, and her voice cracked slightly as she continued. "Honestly, I'm really not sure how it's even happening…"

"You're a hybrid," Verre interrupted. "That's why Madame Rose thought you were so special and why Pan was so dodgy about you."

Cerise sighed in relief. "So you already knew."

Hybrid?

Cerise was a hybrid? It all made sense now. Rage blossomed in her chest, growing into an inferno that made it hard to breathe.

"You must not know Verre very well," Baen said. "It is extremely difficult to keep a secret from her. But if it's any comfort, I was unaware."

"Of course you were." Verre rolled her eyes. "For someone so brilliant, you do miss a lot that happens right under your nose."

Before the two could break out in a fight, Aura spoke up. "I don't hate you, Cerise. Technically we're all outlaws here anyway, since none of us are approved magic-wielders"

"Here, here!" Baen lifted an invisible glass, as if in a toast. "Brilliantly put, Aura. The law is a foolish one as it bans some absolutely wonderful people. You can't help being born with magic"

Verre smiled and glanced at Cerise. "Agreed. Your new abilities will also be extremely useful as we try and find the slippers."

Everyone turned to Blanca, as if expecting her to mirror what they had just stated. She glanced at Cerise, hatred boiling within her.

They were wrong, hybrids were wrong, her mother's death had been wrong. But if she didn't agree with them, it would make it all the harder to complete Madame Rose's task. She would never get the chance to save Lyra and Rose, her only family left.

"You're right, there's nothing wrong with being a hybrid." It felt like she was betraying her mother's memory by saying that. It felt so incredibly wrong. But Lyra's face burned in her mind. She could do this.

Cerise blushed and smiled, ducking her head. "Thank you all," she said simply.

"On the subject of the slippers," Aura continued, fidgeting nervously. "I may have a lead on that. I now know why none who have searched for the slippers have ever returned."

217

Blanca's blood ran cold.

"I saw the slippers. They were around Cevata's neck. The slippers were never buried somewhere on the mountain; they were given to one of the most powerful beings in Atulau—an Ancient One."

24

AURA

VERR WAS THE first to rouse from her shock. "Cevata? The Ancient One? You're saying she has the slippers? You've seen them?"

Aura nodded, knowing how absolutely absurd it sounded. But it was true.

It made sense. The Ancient Ones were the most powerful beings in Atulau. If anyone could be trusted to protect the slippers, it was one of them. But how were the girls supposed to get the slippers? Was it even possible?

"Well, this definitely complicates things. I've never heard of anyone killing an Ancient One." Verre went silent as she thought. "Killing her would be the most effective method, but is it even possible?"

"I agree, but if it turns out she can't be killed…" Cerise didn't need to continue.

"Maybe Blanca's poison will work, but again, if it doesn't, there's no hope for success." Verre went quiet as she thought, brows furrowed.

Cerise cleared her throat and stood. "So it sounds like murder is off the table, but we need magic. How about Aura? Even if Cevata is immortal, I'm sure she still sleeps."

"Excellent idea. And then we can have Blanca kill Cevata. If she's asleep, she can't fight if it doesn't work," Verre said.

"Hold on, we can't just kill Cevata!" Aura's stomach churned in disgust. How could they speak so callously of murder? And besides, could she even will sleep upon Cevata? It was true that her powers would not be harmful to the dragon, so they might actually work on the magical creature. But if Blanca managed to kill Cevata while she was sleeping, and if Aura decided to help... could she live with the knowledge that she helped murder an Ancient One?

"If you had to choose between killing Cevata or killing your family, which would you choose?" Verrre's steely eyes locked with Aura's.

Put that way, it wasn't even a question. Her family always came first. But wasn't there another alternative?

"I think Cerise is right," Aura began tentatively. "My powers should be able to work on a dragon, but I won't know for sure unless I'm next to her. But isn't there an option where we don't have to murder her?"

"If I may," Baen began, "what if Cerise goes and asks for guidance with her magic, and Aura accompanies her, since the dragon seems to have taken a liking to her? The rest of us will wait here, that way we don't raise any suspicions. Us being there won't do anything but potentially injure their chances."

It was a shaky plan at best, but it was the best they had. Aela and Aerik would die if Aura didn't succeed. They had already spent over a week on the mountains, and the longer it took, the more likely it was that they already were.

"Bring your weapons, though," Verre said. "They've been useless to us up until now, but who knows? If things don't go as planned, the best thing you can do is try to fight your way out. As for the plan, I think it has the highest chance of success."

"I agree with you," Aura said. "It's the only somewhat doable plan that might work. If we don't act now, we might as well all be dead."

"Same here; I'm willing to risk it. Is everyone in agreement?" Cerise looked over everyone as both Verre and Blanca nodded. "Very well. Aura and I will leave tomorrow morning at sunrise. Everyone else remains here, and if you see or hear anything that might be a dragon, run. I refuse to sacrifice any more lives than necessary."

It was colder outside than Aura remembered, but it could also have been overwhelming fear that chilled her bones. It was utterly ridiculous of her to try to make a powerful dragon fall asleep so that she could steal a pair of slippers from around its neck.

Absolutely insane.

But she would personally leap into Cevata's mouth if it meant that Aela and Aerik would live. They were her world now that her parents were gone, and she needed to protect them.

"This is insane, isn't it? We're fools," Cerise muttered, burrowing her chapped hands deeper into her pockets, her double-bladed axe hanging from a belt. "I know we're doing this for our families, but have we ever stopped to consider what other people Madame Rose might kill should she get the slippers? We've been told the slippers are extremely powerful, so what's to say she won't use them to destroy Allegora?"

Aura had thought about it, but she couldn't allow her mind to dwell on it. She was saving her siblings, and that was all she cared about. She wouldn't be able to live with herself if she knew the reason her siblings had died was because she had chosen the many over them.

"According to legend, the slippers will only work for Dorthea. Everyone else burns in the blackest of flames." Still, as she said it, there was an odd thought at the back of her head that she couldn't quite bring to mind. Surely Madame Rose knew about the curse of the slippers? Then why was she so set on having them?

"Madame Rose must know that, so why is she putting so much effort into finding them?" Cerise halted and frowned, turning her gaze to Aura.

"Maybe…" Aura swallowed nervously as a thought came to her. "Maybe the slippers aren't Dorthea's. Think about it. Madame Rose has been in Denthlire for centuries without dying. She has to have magic. Maybe the slippers are actually Madame Rose's."

Cerise's eyes widened. "Pan mentioned back in Denthlire that it used to be a prosperous kingdom. A kingdom ruled by a *queen*. Apparently, Dorthea and the mages from Allegora came and destroyed everything."

Was Cerise saying that Madame Rose was Queen of Denthlire? "That's ridiculous," Aura stated weakly. "You don't know for certain. Maybe Madame Rose just doesn't know about the curse on the slippers.

"But what if I *am* right?" Cerise stepped towards Aura, grabbing her fiercely by the shoulders. "What if we're actually making the biggest mistake? If she's really the creator of the slippers, she could do anything with them."

The pieces all fit together, acid roiling in Aura's stomach. "She's Queen of Denthlire," Aura whispered, still not quite believing it.

"We can't give them to her!" Cerise exclaimed. "If she gets them, the world ends. Dorthea is no longer alive, the dragons have all but disappeared—there's no one to combat her! Aura, if she gets those slippers, it's all over."

Aura had no intention of listening to Cerise. Her family's lives were on the line, and she would always choose them over everything else. She had to give the slippers to Madame Rose.

Perhaps Madame Rose would spare her and her siblings since she would be the one to get the slippers. Maybe she would even let them live out their days in some peaceful forest. She couldn't be that evil, right? She would show compassion. Aura *had* to believe that.

"You're right, we can't give them to her, but we can't let Cevata keep them. We'll retrieve the slippers and bring them back to everyone else, and we'll explain. From there, we can create a plan," Aura said, the lie coming far too easily.

Cerise nodded, drawing her cloak close to her face. "Sounds fine to me. Maybe we can re-hide the slippers so that no one will ever be able to find them, or throw them into a volcano, or something. Once we do that, we can ambush Pan and kill him, that way Madame Rose will be helpless."

The thought was tempting, but it rested on the fact of Pan being killable, and she wasn't sure he was. He was odd, with such incredible healing that it was even hard to try and instill sleep in him. Most people's minds welcomed the thought of sleep, but not his, making it extremely difficult to even try. It was too great of a risk.

"Yes, re-hiding them sounds like the proper plan," Aura agreed, clenching her fists tightly at her sides. "Though is Pan able to be killed? He managed to evade injury from each of us, even Verre and Blanca. Maybe he's immortal." The thought was alarming, especially considering his fighting abilities, and only furthered Aura's resolve that she needed to carry out Madame Rose's command.

They trekked through the snow in silence, Aura having developed a hatred of the cold. Everything was miserable and made her wet and freezing. Hadn't the mountains ever heard of sunshine?

Aura longed for warmth. A place that wasn't as oppressively hot as Oobay but wasn't as numbingly cold as the Bluefrost Mountains. Her body was too delicate for either extreme, as much as she hated to admit it. Even if she was healthy, her body was naturally small and light, a trait she had received from her father. Cerise was short as well but had more pronounced curves and a sturdier frame. She was strong.

"Do you think Cevata can really help me with my mage powers?" Cerise asked, breaking the silence. "I had always known of the amazing things my father could do, but I never thought I'd be able to do them myself.

"He was an Elementalist, given one of the rare mage gifts. He could make plants grow or start a fire in our fireplace. He had also created a waterfall when he and I went for a swim in a river one time. It was such a beautiful and unique gift. I just hope mine is the same."

Aura could understand the wish to honor her father's memory. Finding any scrap of parchment he could scavenge, her own father had loved to write stories. Stories of dragons who didn't fly but rather swam in the murky waters of the Evanscenian ocean, or of faeries that delivered wonderful dreams to children.

Aura would sit in fascination as he spoke of daring conquests, gruesome battles, and beautiful love that stood the test of time. He made their small shack of a home seem like a fortress that had withstood the blows of a thousand warriors, or an underwater mansion where the naiads lived. She blamed him for her big dreams, dreams that were too often crushed by the withering demon that was Oobay.

"It makes sense that you're anxious about your gift. I'm sure it will be an amazing one, one that would have made your father proud. Cevata is wise, and I'm sure you'll be able to discover something."

Cerise's wide grin almost made Aura regret what she was going to do. Almost, but not quite. "In the meantime, let's not forget why we're really doing this."

"Agreed. I think we're close enough now," Cerise said quietly, her eyes alert. "Shall I call her, or do you want to?"

"I can," Aura said, trying to hide how nervous a second confrontation with the dragon made her. Maybe if she wasn't about to steal from her, it would be less nerve-wracking.

Standing as straight as she could, she cupped her hands over her mouth and called, "Cevata!"

Aura watched the clear skies above, heart pounding. Then, a great storm whirled in from their left bringing with it a cold that settled deep into Aura's very soul.

"Aura, Cerise," a loud voice purred, causing the ground to rumble. "What a pleasure."

CERISE

IT HAD BEEN one thing to stand from a distance and gaze at Cevata, but it was entirely another to stand so close that Cerise was able to see the design in each scale.

It was absolutely terrifying.

But she was also excited. Now she would finally be able to carry on her father's legacy of being a mage. She would also be one of the first were-mages, something she believed would make her mother proud.

"You wish for help in unlocking your abilities as a mage? Interesting, though I can't say I'm surprised. I knew from the moment I saw you that you were special. The union between a mage and any other being is rare, and a union between a mage and werewolf has only ever been heard of once before. I can help with making your abilities available to you, but you must do all the work in developing them. Is that clear?" Cevata raised an eyebrow and stared solemnly at Cerise.

There was so much wisdom and power hidden behind those dark eyes like pools of blackest ink. Was she ready for these powers? Sometimes she couldn't even control the one she had now. Still, if the power resided within her, shouldn't she explore it? Discover what she could do? "Yes, I understand what is expected of me."

Cevata nodded approvingly. "Very well, but be warned: you have within you much more power than you can possibly realize. It might overwhelm you."

Her stomach dropped. Would it consume her like the wolf had? What if she could not control it?

Perhaps it wasn't wise though she desperately wanted it. It was a lot to consider. Maybe her new abilities could help combat Pan and Madame Rose. Maybe they could help them win.

Cevata studied her gravely. "You're not certain. If you're not fully settled on this, I will not help you. One who doubts can be dangerous. Tell me now: are you ready?"

Her father would have believed in her, would have told her to seize this chance that she had been given. "I am certain. This is what I want and what my father would have wanted too. I'm ready." Cerise stood tall, managing to look Cevata straight in the eyes.

"Very well." Cevata nodded. "I shall do as you requested."

She exhaled, freezing air surrounding Cerise. It was palpable, heavy with magic. Pain seared through Cerise's mind, causing her to whimper. Was it supposed to hurt? Something within her fought the ice, making the pain increase. It was a battle in her mind, each side pulling at her to retreat to them. She dropped to the ground, feeling like she was frozen solid. She had to be made of ice at this point.

Suddenly, it was over. Cerise let out a ragged breath, her vision clearing.

Aura stood just to her right, her eyes wide with fear. "I thought you had died for a moment. First you twitched, then your skin turned blue, then suddenly you lay still. Are you alright?"

Cerise rose slowly, her limbs shaking. Was she hurt? Her head pounded still, but the rest of her body felt oddly rejuvenated. Even the headache began to lessen. "Yes, I'm fine. In fact, I feel great." She turned in wonder to Cevata.

"It is a sub-product of my magic. It heals as well as destroys. Your father had placed quite the impressive spell on your mind, a dampener for your powers. I'm sorry it was so painful."

Her father had placed a dampening spell on her? Was that why it had taken so long to show signs of magic?

It was like she had been punched in the stomach, filling her with an aching hollowness. She couldn't understand why her father wouldn't have wanted her to have magical abilities just like him. Maybe he had been afraid of what a were-mage could do? Maybe he had been protecting her? Cerise wished she knew, but he was gone now.

"What exactly are my abilities, Cevata? I know I can shift into a wolf and that I can detect mage spells, but what else can I do?" Already she could feel a tingling surge move through her body. Was that magic?

"You can do so much more than that," Cevata chuckled, cold air escaping her mouth. "Both your mother and your father's abilities were amplified in you. What kind of mage was your father?"

"He was an Elementalist," Cerise said eagerly.

A shadow passed over Cevata's face. "Interesting. The Elementalists are quite powerful. Mage magic works through bloodlines, so your mage magic will match your father's, meaning life, light, and dark magic are not yours to control. Thankfully, the differences between fire, earth, air, and water are relatively easy to distinguish between. Simply listen for their song."

Cerise frowned. "What does that even mean? Magic doesn't have a song."

A blast of cold air hit her face, and Cevata growled deep in her throat. "Do not doubt the intricacies of magic! Now, close your eyes."

Tensing her legs to fight the tremble that went through them, Cerise did as Cevata said.

"Search deep inside of yourself. Past your fears, your doubts, your demons. What is the song your soul sings?"

Cerise felt her cheeks warm with shame. Cevata might be a powerful dragon, but she sounded like a raving lunatic. What did Aura think of all of this? Cerise risked a glance at her, but clamped her eyes shut again as Cevata snarled.

"If you will not humble yourself, I will not help. Understood?"

Scolding herself, Cerise nodded. She could do this. Just listen for the song of her soul. As she relaxed, a buzz filled her bones.

What was her song?

The forest of Lithrium came to mind. The green canopy overhead. The strength of the wood. The unyielding stone. The resilience of the ground.

"Resilience," she whispered. "My song is resilience."

"Very good," Cevata purred. "Your element is earth."

The element earth. The memory of her father creating a blooming flower came rushing back. Could she make the earth shake and boulders move? Could she make flowers bloom or wither and die?

"What about my mother?" she asked, a nervous smile on her face.

"Werewolves are powerful, primal creatures, but magically, their only power is shape-shifting. Given that your father was a mage, I'd assume your shape-shifting is much broader now, including creatures outside of wolves. But you must test that," Cevata said.

Shifting had been something Cerise had always hated because of the lack of control, but what if she could shift into beings that weren't dangerous? Something that wasn't a monster?

Focusing on Aura, she forced her body to shift as it normally did, determined to keep that image of Aura in the front of her mind. Her body shortened and narrowed. Glancing down, she realized that her skin had changed from its usual warm brown to pale white. Her enchanted clothes had changed size with her, fitting to her smaller body.

"Wow, this is so odd." She gasped in fright, realizing that she had Aura's voice as well. "I feel like I'm still me, but I'm not. I look just like you, Aura." She glanced at Aura, who had backed away.

"It's too strange, seeing myself. Can you shift back? Please." Cerise didn't blame Aura for being disturbed. It was strange for her too.

Concentrating, she shifted back, feeling much more comfortable in her own body. Still, shifting into something new under *her* control was exhilarating. Euphoria rushed through her, and the pain was hardly noticeable.

Cevata watched her with amusement. "It will take time getting used to these new abilities, so use them sparingly. Just like you wouldn't immediately sprint after an illness, you shouldn't try to test the limits of your abilities from the start. Let yourself grow accustomed to them."

It made sense that she should allow herself time to adjust, for she still had no idea the limits of her abilities.

But she had to experiment once more.

Allowing herself to feel the ground below her—a curious buzz filling her bones—she could sense everything. The dirt, the creatures that hid beneath it, the boulders buried deep, the cold underground river that swept by furiously. She could feel all of it, and the ground, the rocks... they seemed to beckon to her to command them.

She reached out her hand, calling for a boulder to rise. For a moment, there was nothing. Then the snow shuddered with a great force, the ground splitting open around her. Rising from the canyon... came a pebble.

Disappointed, she dropped the pebble, watching it clatter down the impressive hole she had created.

Booming laughter followed. Stinging with shame, Cerise turned to Cevata, whose chuckles only grew louder, shaking the snow off of the nearby trees.

"That might have been the most amusing thing I've witnessed these last few centuries," Cevata wheezed, releasing a large sigh, the cold air brushing by Cerise's curls.

"You find it easy to destroy, so that's why the crater you have now left in my mountain is rather large, but you had some trouble commanding, and I doubt creating would come easily to you. But it's all in your nature. Your mother's more dominant traits must have been passed along in you, giving you the desire to destroy and command, as opposed to create and cultivate."

Cerise nodded, still too humiliated to answer. A pebble? All that effort, and a pebble! She had expected to be great at wielding her earth powers, same as her shifting ones. It was a tough truth to swallow that she wasn't as competent with magic as she had wished.

Hearing a low snicker, she turned to Aura, who had a grin on her face. Cheeks flaming, she ducked her head. The last thing she needed at the moment was Aura laughing at her.

"Do not be ashamed—it's perfectly natural to fail a few times before succeeding. If you consider it, you did make the ground split open and did command that rock to come toward you. The last person I taught to use their mage abilities couldn't even manipulate a drop of water for the first few days. It takes time."

"Who was the last person you taught? Were they a mage?" Cerise hadn't known that Cevata had taught other mages. But to be fair, she hadn't even known that there were dragons in Allegora until just a few days ago, for Evanscene's sake!

"Her name was Dorthea—the only other were-mage hybrid I've ever known. I'm sure you've heard of her. That's why I warned you of your powers; the last hybrid I taught tore apart the world," Cevata said quietly.

Dorthea had been a hybrid? *She had been like me?* The thought was dumbfounding. She had always held her in such high esteem, and to now know she was a hybrid too?

"I never knew that. She was a hero to the people of Allegora."

"Yes," Cevata sighed, "she was. But the king of the time was afraid of her and what she could do. Dorthea was the reason hybrids were made illegal.

"Over time, people forgot she had been anything but a mage, and they considered her a hero, never once realizing that she was the very thing they were afraid of. That was why I was wary of... " Her eyelids fluttered, her words slurring. "I... " A yawn, followed by the drooping of her eyes. She never finished, awkwardly slumping to the ground in sleep.

Cerise whirled around, spotting Aura who crouched on the ground. "She was so incredibly strong," Aura said, catching her breath. "If she had placed any magical shields against my abilities, I wouldn't have been able to do anything." She rose slowly, making her way to Cevata.

"Hurry! I don't know how long the sleep will last, but we need to be gone by then."

Cerise was stunned, feeling awful for having taken advantage of such a kind being. She had helped Cerise so incredibly much. But this was about survival and saving those she loved. About saving everyone.

There, practically embedded in the dragon's scales, were the slippers. Cerise didn't know what she had expected, but these weren't it. The slippers had no heel, and looked extremely durable. They weren't a shimmering red, either, but a deep, pulsing red, like blood from a freshly slain kill.

Cerise stumbled back as the spells flashed across her mind. *A spell of shielding, of pain, of blood, of death. A spell to prevent drowning.* There were so many spells and too much power. She flinched, closing her eyes against the onslaught of words that invaded her mind.

Aura carefully removed the slippers, dropping them with a yelp. The slippers sizzled in the snow, then stopped. Aura gingerly picked them up again, relief shining on her face. "We have them."

Cerise was going to respond, but she felt heavy, like a thousand stones weighed down her body. Perhaps she should rest a moment, just lay down in the soft snow.

Her eyes snapped open, and she jerked herself upright.

Aura was trying to make her sleep!

Focusing all of her concentration on shifting, she became a wolf. But it was already too late. Her body crashed into the snow as her eyes slowly closed.

VERRE

IT WAS ONLY the second time Verre had ever thrown up, the first having been after eating twenty sourbuds on a dare.

Staggering back into the cave, her stomach still churning, she eased herself down. Her only chance at a midday nap so far on this trip, and now it was ruined. What was wrong with her? It wasn't like her to get jittery during a mission. Was it nerves? Perhaps she was worried about Cerise and Aura. They were so young, after all. Maybe she should have joined them.

"Verre?" Baen half-rose from where he had been resting beside her. "Are you alright? You're looking especially pale." He placed an arm around her waist, pulling her toward him. She didn't resist, enjoying the added warmth and nearness it brought.

"I'm fine, really. I—" Were those tears welling up in her eyes? She never cried. What was wrong with her?

Swallowing hard—and commanding the tears to remain in her eyes—she continued, "I'm just tired, is all. It has been an exhausting month trying to survive and make sure everyone else does too."

One month. Had it already been that long since she had last seen her parents or slept in her own bed? The thought made her homesick, and she almost cried... again. Instead of crying, though, she ran outside and vomited... again.

"Verre, there is definitely something wrong. You never *ever* throw up." Baen had rushed out after her without a cloak or anything. He was going to freeze to death worrying about her. "Let's get you back inside so I can figure out what in Denthlire is happening."

Thankfully, Blanca had gone on a walk. Her normal breath was barely toxic, but the longer she spent in the cave, the worse it got. She also said she preferred to be by herself, so no one minded when she went on little strolls.

Settling back down on the patch of ground that served as her bed, Verre let out a deep breath, her entire being frazzled.

A sneaking suspicion began to dawn on her as Baen massaged her shoulders in an attempt of comfort. When had her last cycle been? It had been before she had been captured, at least a month before that, actually. The more she considered it, the more it made sense. A horrible, fear-instilling sort of sense.

It was—unfortunately—highly probable that she was, in fact, pregnant.

But she couldn't be pregnant, not now. She and Baen had always talked about having children, to one day start a family, but now was the literal worst time to be pregnant. How could she carry out what she needed to while carrying a baby?

There was a chance she was wrong. Still, as she rested her hand subtly on her stomach, she couldn't help the flood of love and excitement this new change brought.

Judging from her cycle, she was at least eight weeks along. But, it was most likely ten or twelve. Still, ten weeks seemed like such a short amount of time, especially since she still had thirty to go.

The rhythmic pressure of Baen's hands on her back brought her back to reality. She couldn't tell Baen. He would sacrifice himself in exchange for her and the baby's safety. And that wouldn't help anyway since Madame Rose would probably just kill her and the baby too.

Still, she wouldn't be able to keep it a secret for long, not with her lean form. She would tell him once the slippers had been safely handed to Madame Rose. Or once Blanca killed Pan, like they had talked about before she'd left on her walk.

She was putting a lot of trust in Blanca by having her do this, but it was crucial that Pan be eliminated. Verre was wary of leaving anyone alive who could best her.

"Baen, what do you want to do once we're done with this infernal commission I'm being forced to execute?" Verre turned around to face him, wondering if she did indeed have a protruding stomach... and hoping she didn't.

Baen didn't seem to notice any difference, thankfully. "I'd like to leave Berth, maybe explore another land or two. Once we're tired of our fun, we can settle back down in Berth, finally claim those titles your parents have been pestering us to take, and have a dozen children." He grinned, pulling her close so that he could place a kiss on her forehead. "And what about you? What do you think we should do?"

Verre thought for a moment, not able to stop obsessing over the fact that he wanted children. Would he be happy that their plans weren't going quite as expected?

"I want to travel too, to enjoy ourselves as long as possible before returning to Berth. But I also want to stop being an assassin. I'm tired of seeing death everywhere I go. I want to experience life." She hesitated, wondering if she should tell him the news after all. "Actually, on the subject of life—"

Aura burst into the cave, a pair of dangling shoes in her hand. "I found them. The slippers, we have them. Everything is going to be alright." Her cheeks were flushed, though from the cold or excitement, Verre couldn't tell. She did notice that Aura came alone, though.

"Where is Cerise? What happened?" Verre demanded, her nausea momentarily forgotten. Despite her initial reservations, she had grown rather fond of the other three. "Why isn't she here?"

Aura backed away. "I had to, I'm sorry. You don't understand, she wanted to destroy the slippers instead of delivering them. She thought the sacrifice was worth it because," she hesitated, "because of who Madame Rose actually is."

"Who is Madame Rose?" Blanca asked quietly, entering the cave. Aura started at the noise, almost dropping the vivid red sippers.

"Madame Rose is Queen of Denthlire," Aura blurted out. "She can wear the slippers because she created them, not Dorthea. That's why Cerise refused to give them to her. I didn't kill her, just made her sleep. Cevata will awake soon too, so we have to hurry!"

The girl was chattering on so fast, it was hard for Verre to follow, except for the detail that Madame Rose was the ruler of Denthlire. Now Verre's theory made even more sense. Dread twisted inside her, but she shoved it down, forcing herself to focus on what this meant for them.

Aura had said that Cerise wanted to destroy the slippers? It was a brilliant idea, but it meant all their loved ones would die. What if she had to choose between Atulau and her family? Could she choose? Glancing over at Baen, she smiled.

Yes, without a question. Baen and her parents would always come first, and now she had a little one to protect as well. Her hand slid over her stomach, realizing she did, in fact, have a small bump. Sure, it was miniscule, hardly more than what an exhale would have created, but Verre couldn't help but treasure the image in her mind.

"You are right; we have to give the slippers to her. We'll figure out how to stop her somehow. Our families are worth more." Verre sighed heavily, guilty for abandoning her homeland and its preservation. They would be able to figure something out, right? They would find a way to kill her.

Baen's hand rested on her shoulder, his eyes hardened with resolve. "Verre, no. You can't choose your parents and me over all of Atulau! You could save so many people if you sacrifice us. Maybe we can rig a trap or something, or we can hide far away where they'll never find us. Please, don't do this."

Verre blinked back tears, crushing Baen in a fierce embrace. "I can't. I refuse to lose you. Not now. You're my world, my love, my jester. I will always choose you, no matter what." She pressed a fevered kiss to his lips, desperate for him to understand. She didn't even care about the other girls or their gawking stares.

Baen wrapped her tightly in his arms, as if afraid to let her go. Verre pulled away, cupping his face in her hands. "Don't you see? I love you too much to let you die."

He looked at her deeply with those beautiful brown eyes of his and smiled. "I know you love me, and there's no one else I'd rather spend my life with. But it would haunt me to know that I was the cause for so many lives lost." Baen pulled away gently. "Let me make this decision, please."

No, no, no. He couldn't leave her. Verre needed him. He needed her. They were one; wife and husband. "I'm pregnant," she stated quickly before she could decide against it. "If you sacrifice yourself, our baby will never know its father, and what if Madame Rose decides I'm too dangerous to keep alive? She'll kill me and the baby."

It was definitely not how she pictured telling him, in a moment of weakness and in front of a crowd, but if it made him stay, she didn't care.

"A baby," Baen echoed slowly, glancing down at her stomach. "A baby! You're pregnant?" An odd look passed over his face, almost like fear. Before Verre could question him, though, he scooped her up into

245

his arms. The adorable grin that replaced the fearful look set Verre's mind at ease.

"But this complicates things," he said, setting her down gently, as if she were glass that might break. The analogy almost made her chuckle. She of all people knew how strong glass could be.

And she was plenty durable, though it was cute to see him so protective. It wasn't like she was a trained killer or anything.

"Yes, it complicates things, but now do you see why we need to give her the slippers? Blanca and I have a plan to kill Pan once he delivers them. I always had a hunch Madame Rose would try to kill us once we'd helped her, but dying was less frightening than the possibility of losing you." Verre glanced over at Blanca, who wouldn't meet her eyes.

"Okay, so then we deliver the slippers, kill Pan, and figure out a way to stay alive. Hm, the odds do seem to be against us, but we can make it work." Baen looked down at her stomach again, as if he couldn't believe they would actually be parents.

"About killing," Blanca whispered, having moved to stand just outside the cave. "I was told by Madame Rose to kill you all once I had procured the slippers. But I can't do it."

She took a shaky breath, wiping away the tears on her face. "I have a baby sister, and all I want to do is protect her. That's why I didn't refuse Madame Rose. But I don't have it in me to kill you, and now I feel like I've failed my little Crescent Rose." Her voice broke.

"But I am going to kill Pan. Maybe I can stop him from retrieving the slippers, and maybe I can save you all. I'm so, so sorry. I will make all of this right in the end, I promise. Just get as far away from here as possible, understood?" She snatched up the slippers as Verre and the rest stared at her in shock. Then she fled.

BLANCA

BLANCA HAD TO do this for them. Hearing Verre announce that she was pregnant had brought back the memory of Lyra telling her the same thing. That half-shy smile that brimmed over with hope was the same on both their faces. She couldn't kill them, even if she wanted to.

Still, she felt like she had betrayed little Rose and Lyra. If she wasn't able to kill Pan, it was all over. She would be dead and everyone with her. It was up to her to keep them all safe.

Up to me.

The thought didn't instill a sense of bravery or nobleness like she would have hoped. In fact, she couldn't believe she had made such a rash decision. But it was too late to second-guess herself.

She hugged the slippers close, determined to keep them out of Pan's grasp. He had always terrified her, but she was different now, more courageous, smarter, and wiser.

Pan had trained her to face every obstacle, right? So he would just be another obstacle in her way. An obstacle that would most likely kill her. I can't think like that. It would take so little for her to run back to the cave, back to safety.

Where they had first been transported to wasn't too far, just a good fifteen minute's walk. Still, it was enough time for Blanca to seriously begin to regret her heroic move.

This was a suicide mission.

Even if she managed to kill Pan, he would most likely injure her in some way. Somehow, the thought of death wasn't as frightening as she would have imagined though her heart still raced and her vision was unfocused.

Every shaky step brought her closer to death. Her throat ached from the cold as she forced oxygen down into...

Blanca shivered in the small, abandoned cottage she had discovered in the woods. It was sturdy, but with no dry wood for the fireplace, it was freezing. She glanced miserably at the dripping wet wood she was trying to dry. They had been hiding for a week now, and Blanca had already used up all the good wood to heat Rose's food.

If she didn't warm the cottage soon, they would both freeze to death. Blanca went over to Rose, who had been sleeping fitfully all day. Their first day away, Blanca had bought a pound of ground bracken, a grain used especially for young children. Blanca hadn't had enough money to buy food for herself. Had it already been eight days since she had last eaten?

She would have cried, but it seemed to take too great an effort. It was also too numbingly cold to think straight.

Blanca had just rested her head on the moldy bed, closing her eyes, when Rose let out a weak wail.

Forcing herself up again, she staggered over to the basket that served as Rose's cradle.

She had soiled her clothes again.

Tears welled up in Blanca's eyes, but she pushed them away. If she was back at home, she might be dead, same as Rose. Her father had finally lost it, and it was no longer safe to live in the manor. Blanca knew that, Lyra knew that, the whole town knew that. He was power- and magic-obsessed, and nothing could change that.

Changing the baby's undergarments as swiftly as possible—her regular breathing turning to panting in the process—she tossed them into the fast-growing pile of laundry.

Rose was running out of things to wear, but there was no soap with which to wash them. After placing the baby back to sleep in the basket, Blanca steeled herself and grabbed the pile of stinking clothes.

Trying not to gag, she hurried to the little stream that ran just outside the cottage. She set the clothes down and picked up a large stick since the stream had frozen over. A few weak jabs broke the ice, allowing the water to run freely. Her head grew light, and Blanca grabbed the embankment for support.

Gritting her teeth against the fog that invaded her brain, Blanca waded in bravely, gasping as the icy water bit into her flesh. In a way, it was almost nice. It woke her up and heightened her senses.

She quickly began to wash the clothes as best she could, placing them to dry on the embankment.

How dismal and dreary these looked compared to the lacy, billowing gowns she used to wear to the palace. Even now she could imagine the airy music and swishing skirts as everyone danced gaily…

The sharp crack of a dead branch caused Blanca to freeze. An old woman stood awkwardly on the embankment across from her, smiling. "Sorry, I didn't mean to frighten you. I didn't know anyone lived here."

Blanca scrambled out of the water, her limbs shaking. "No need to apologize. I was just startled. What brings you into the forest?" She finished wringing out the clothes, heaping them into her arms. Whoever the woman was, Blanca didn't trust her.

"Can I help you with those?" The woman gingerly took the clothes, grimacing as water seeped into her ragged apparel. "And how about an apple?" She carefully pulled it out of her pocket. It was lovely—bright red and shiny. Blanca almost

251

drooled just looking at it. "Here, you should have it. A perfect apple for a perfect young lady." She smiled a toothless grin.

Blanca took it hesitantly, unsure if it was wise to. Still, her stomach was ravenous for food; it begged for it. One apple couldn't hurt, right?

"Go on, take a bite. I can practically see your ribs through that gown," she said, shifting the clothes in her arms.

Just a bite, she promised herself as she bit into the apple. It was delicious, the crisp skin giving way to firm flesh.

Her taste buds nearly exploded with the tangy sweetness.

But then it turned sour and sent a crawling sensation down her throat, like hundreds of tiny spiders in a frantic attempt at escape. Her eyes grew wide as she tried to choke it out, but it remained lodged in her throat. Chills swept over her body as she fell to the ground, the apple falling from her hand.

Darkness crept at the corners of her vision as her father glanced down at her, laughing maniacally. Then it all disappeared.

Blanca grabbed at a nearby tree, still able to feel the spiders in her throat. She shuddered, the memory one she wished she could forget again.

So it had been her father who had killed her. He had tricked her, poisoned her. She knew she should be used to disappointment from him, but... *Who kills their own flesh and blood?*

Now she wasn't sure what had happened to Rose. Had he killed her too? Had he taken her back to the manor to live out a life of disappointment and abuse?

Despite the grief it brought her to consider what might have happened to Lyra and Rose, she couldn't dwell on that now. She had a promise to fulfill. If she thought about it any longer, many people would die. She was tired of living around violence, blood, and death. So she pressed on, plowing through the snow.

He had killed her. Her own father. The thought echoed over and over in her head, but she forced it into silence. Right now she was far too busy just trying to keep the nervous roiling of her stomach to a minimum.

It only took a short while to reach the first spot from which she had seen the land of Allegora stretched out below.

Too short.

She lingered for a moment, enjoying the still-rising sun and the warmth it brought her. She knew she might not survive to see another sunrise. The thought caused her stomach to tighten with worry.

"Pan?" she called, glancing around. Her voice was shaky, so she cleared her throat and continued.

"I have the slippers, just as Madame Rose requested. My family will be safe now, correct?" She spoke as loudly as possible, watching with satisfaction as green mist billowed around her. "I know you're here somewhere, watching me. Please, come take the slippers. I have done as you have asked."

There was a light whoosh, and there was Pan, backing away as quickly as possible.

Blanca watched in fascination as his skin began to melt, exposing the red flesh beneath. But the injury slowly closed up, and he frowned.

"Blanca, you know your breath is toxic. Come, just give me the slippers, and I'll be on my way. Madame Rose will reward you for your cooperation."

He thought she was nothing but a silly little girl, which reassured her. He didn't think her capable of killing him.

"How dare you!" she screamed, savoring the rage and pure loudness of it. "You have threatened to take my loved ones away. You would have murdered a child! A child!"

Pan scrambled away, legitimate fear in his eyes. "Blanca, let's discuss this." His skin began to peel back, blood seeping down his arms. He teleported directly behind her, grabbing the slippers, but the poison was too much. He dropped them, falling to the ground coughing.

"No! I'm done agreeing with everyone else. I am finally making my own decisions, and no one, not even you, can tell me otherwise."

Her throat was hoarse, but she didn't care. With every word, her poison grew, growing so thick it killed the trees that were anywhere near her. She was taking control of her own life now. And while she was still terrified, it was exhilarating.

She watched as Pan tried to teleport away from the mountainside, but he kept popping back in the same place. Judging by the fear on his face, he wasn't doing it on purpose.

"Rose!" he screamed, flinging his head up, the poison continuing its work. "This is against the contract! You can't force me to stay!"

But he was unable to teleport away.

Desperate, Pan whipped out a knife, flinging it expertly at her. She gasped, feeling the cold metal invade her body. It hurt, worse than she had thought possible. Fingers trembling, she wrapped them around the handle, feeling sticky wetness touch her skin.

The knife was embedded deep within her abdomen. She wanted to remove it, but her job wasn't complete yet. She could do this; she had to.

Staggering, she inhaled deeply and screamed, "You are a monster, nothing but a nightmare that only lasts a night! You think you're strong, but your strength only lies in your physical abilities. You think I'm nothing but a weak and silly girl. I have been through things you can't even dream of; I've suffered from trauma you can't even imagine. I have literally died and been brought back to life. I will not stand by and let another monster dictate my life. I'm done with that."

Her voice sank to a whisper, but it didn't matter. Pan was dead. Her poison had spread throughout the entire mountainside, killing everything in sight. His skull was blackened, the flesh melted and stripped away. What had once scared her was nothing but a skeleton now.

She sank to the ground, blood spilling from around the dagger. Her breath came in short gasps, the pain making her delirious.

"All I ever wanted was to make you proud, Father. I simply wanted you to look at me with love and say 'daughter.' Why didn't you love me? Was it because of Mother? I didn't know the old man who gave me flowers was a hybrid, I didn't know. Please, Father, it wasn't my fault Mother died." Tears spilled from her eyes as she closed them, her breathing evening out. "I just wanted you to be proud."

Then, a moment of clarity. This had been her role to play. It wasn't natural to be brought back to life, to live twice. It was time for her to be reunited with her mother, wherever that might be.

She eased herself down into the snow, her fingers grasping the handle again. With one painful pull, the blade came free, slick with her blood.

Already she was too weak to hold it, and it dropped from her fingers, staining the snow to her right. She could feel the life draining from her body for the second time.

Blanca had done it; she had stopped Pan. Now they would all be safe, hopefully even little Rose. "I'm coming home, Mother," she whispered, the poison slowly fading away around her.

28

AURA

"WE HAVE TO leave now," Aura said quickly, piling her things into her pack. "If Blanca doesn't succeed, we'll all be dead within a matter of minutes." Why did she have to go and ruin Aura's plan? What if Aela and Aerik died now because of her?

Even so, her heart wrenched at the thought of Blanca sacrificing herself. How many people would have to die before this would be over?

"We can't just leave Blanca," Verre protested, scanning the hillside. "She's risking her very life for us. We should be helping her!"

Baen grabbed her shoulder gently, enveloping her in a quick hug. "I understand, but Blanca is risking her life to save us. The best thing we can do is honor her wishes by escaping. Come on, grab your things. Aura is right. We need to move as quickly as possible."

Aura shouldered her pack, looking down at Cerise's that rested in the corner. Guilt wormed its way through her. Had she been right in leaving her? Shaking the thought away, she left Cerise's pack, just in case she managed to make it back to the cave. There was no time to try to find her. If Blanca failed, they'd all be dead soon enough.

"Alright, everyone ready to go?" Verre slung her pack over her shoulder, giving one last wistful glance to the surrounding landscape.

Aura couldn't help but notice the slight bump—and it really was small—that appeared when Verre's shirt was pulled tight. It was odd. She had never seen Verre as the motherly type, though she hadn't seen her as someone who would marry, either.

It went to show that appearances weren't everything, and that people were much more than what they allowed others to see.

Blanca was no exception. In the end, she had risked everything to help them, even though she initially was told to kill them. Aura respected her for that.

As they walked swiftly and silently through the snow, Aura realized that she didn't mind the cold as much. It had taken her over a week, but she was finally growing accustomed to it. It was doubtful that she'd ever find it pleasant, but she didn't constantly think about how cold it was anymore.

She dreaded returning to Oobay, if she could even make it that far. Still, the thought of Aela and Aerik running into her arms was enough for her to long for the dirty shack that she had called home for the past four years.

It was odd—life in Oobay seemed like a lifetime ago. The heat, the poverty, the hope to get just one meal a day. She had almost forgotten what it was like to be starving, though not quite. It was impossible to completely forget that aching emptiness that would spread from her abdomen to the rest of her body, the absolute fatigue that would overwhelm her, making her numb except for the pain that never left her stomach.

Aura had changed since that time. She was bolder now, more sure of herself. She had looked some of the most dangerous beings in the eye and had lived. No matter what happened next, she was ready for it. She was a survivor.

Her fingers grasped the dagger at her side, the one she hadn't used yet. She had been certain that by now it would have been bathed in blood at least once, but thankfully it was not. Would she have the will to kill someone purposefully? To take away their life? She knew Cerise had killed, and Verre definitely had, but could she?

It made her stomach squirm to think of piercing someone with her dagger, watching their life drain away. Violence wasn't something she was comfortable with. Even back in Oobay, she hadn't hurt anyone unless absolutely necessary, and that was only when her siblings had been threatened.

Her abilities weren't meant for killing; they didn't even harm. They simply gave others sleep, which was beneficial in the moment, but eventually just rejuvenated her enemies. But if her loved ones were threatened...

Aura remembered the one man who had tried to steal Aela. He had been at least twenty, obviously a factory worker. Aura had been away searching for food when she heard the screams. No one else had cared, for children were taken all the time and the screams were an everyday occurrence, but Aura had known whose screams they were. She had never been so afraid yet so furious.

Running as fast as she could go, she had come upon the man, filthy, with a delighted grin on his face. He had held Aela tightly by her arm, her braids having come undone. Her face was red from crying.

Before Aura could react or even do anything, Aerik had appeared, swinging a large metal bar. It had connected with the man's knee, causing him to yelp in surprise and pain. He had then snatched Aerik as well, dragging the kids away.

That had been the first and only time Aura's powers had come close to killing someone. She remembered focusing all of her power on him, ripping into his mind. She allowed her mind force to utterly destroy his.

She projected all of her anger, frustration, and fear into him. The man didn't have a chance and dropped to the ground, babbling like a maniac.

That night she hadn't been able to sleep.

Her blood ran hot at the thought of the man as she adjusted the straps of her satchel. He never healed after what she did. Any sense had left his brain for good, and within days he had been taken by the hooded ones.

She hadn't intended to hurt him; all she had wanted was to make him sleep like anyone else. But deep down she had realized that at that moment, she hadn't cared what happened to him. She only cared about Aela and Aerik.

And if that were to ever happen again, Aura would not hesitate. Even to kill, no matter how guilty it might make her. She would give up everything for her siblings.

"What's that?" Baen asked, glancing up the mountainside, his voice thick with worry. "Is that what I think it is?"

Aura followed his gaze, fear settling in the pit of her stomach. It was a fog. Green, fast-approaching fog.

It was Blanca.

Her battle with Pan must have begun, but her poison was rapidly spreading much farther than normal. If this was what it would look like if Blanca spoke normally and more often, she truly was terrifying.

Trees withered and died, becoming blackened husks. Creatures of all kinds scampered wildly, trying to flee the mist that sped toward them.

"Hurry! Stop staring at it like idiots; we need to run!" Verre began to sprint down the sloping ground, surprisingly graceful in calf-deep snow. Baen and Aura followed suit, hoping to beat the mist that was creeping toward them.

The land was eerily quiet, all life either dead or busy running. The silence sent goosebumps scampering up her arms and she couldn't shake the feeling of dread that spread through her body.

After a few minutes, Aura's legs began to ache, her body still not healthy enough for prolonged periods of strenuous exercise. Her breath came in short gasps as she willed her legs to move faster. It didn't help that Verre and Baen were both much taller, their long legs pounding through the snow with ease.

Sweat began to form on her face and her body, soaking through on her back. Even though it was freezing, she removed her cloak, the cold air helping revive her. They ran for what felt like hours but was probably only ten minutes. Aura stumbled, just barely catching herself.

Glancing back, she saw that the poison was far behind them but still too close for comfort.

She didn't allow herself to stop, not yet. Her legs would most likely lock up if she did. Her black hair was plastered against her neck, and she was hot as she kept going. She would soon be freezing with all the sweat that poured off her body.

Seeing Verre and Baen slowing down ahead, she came to a stop herself, her legs giving out beneath her. The snow was a welcome pillow, cradling her overworked body. But as she had predicted, she soon grew cold.

Verre came to crouch beside her, her breathing much less heavy and sporadic, and handed her a cloak. "Put this on. I refuse to have you die on me after we've come so far. And I'm impressed with how well you ran. Especially with your health and size. It was a wonder Baen or I didn't have to carry you." Verre smiled. "Nicely done."

The next moment she was hurrying away, vomiting once more into the snow. Aura had almost forgotten Verre was pregnant. This must have been especially hard for her, what with her nausea and exhaustion. Yet, she had still managed to keep up with Baen. Verre was the toughest person she knew, and Aura was glad to have her with them.

Baen rubbed Verre's back soothingly. "You did great, darling. It's alright that you're feeling nauseous. I read a book on childbirth—rather gruesome, really—and discovered that vomiting, fatigue, and odd food cravings are completely normal. It's astonishing that you're still able to do so much. And look, we're far enough away. The poison can't reach us here."

Verre just nodded, looking more worn out than Aura had ever seen her. She even allowed Baen to take her into his arms.

Pulling the cloak on, Aura smiled. This was a side of Baen that she had never seen. Granted, she had only known him for a few days, but she knew him as a light-hearted, teasing man. He was witty and hilarious and quite good-looking too.

But right now, he reminded her of her father. He would always hold her mother like that if it had been a hard day at the factories. He would softly comb through her hair, humming a song that they considered 'theirs.' It made her heart ache to see another couple acting the same way.

Glancing back up the blackened mountainside, Aura wondered if there was any way the poison hadn't killed Pan. Before moving on, they would remain for a few days at another cave Cerise had discovered. If Blanca didn't join them in that amount of time... Well, Aura didn't want to consider that.

The poison was dissipating, leaving behind the marks of its destruction. Trees were now skeletons. Creatures were simply dark splotches in the snow, too still to be anything but dead. Aura swallowed down the bile that burned in the back of her throat.

Blanca had to have defeated him.

They walked slowly the remainder of the way to the cave, Aura's legs aching by the time they reached it. They were all unusually somber, simply staring with blank expressions at the fire Verre started.

Shouldn't they all be happy? They had survived! But surviving wasn't the same thing as thriving, and Aura had been surviving for far too long. If Blanca had failed, it meant death for everyone. All their work, all their suffering, all those nights of wondering if their families were still alive. All of it would be for nothing.

They were all split apart too. Cerise was somewhere on the mountain, and Blanca still hadn't returned. It gave Aura an uneasy feeling.

Was this all there was? Search a mountain, find some slippers, and kill Pan? Madame Rose was defeated that easily?

No, those slippers were meant to reach Madame Rose, and Aura had the horrible feeling that they would, and that Blanca's sacrifice... She shut her eyes tightly.

She didn't want to believe it. She wanted to believe that her fear was invalid, but she couldn't.

A thunderclap sounded, echoing so loudly that Aura covered her ears. But there hadn't been lightning. She scrambled up, glancing up at the cloudy sky above.

It was red—a deep, blood red that made Aura shudder. The clouds had veins of black running through them, eerily similar to lightning.

But these didn't move.

Another boom came, this one strong enough to shake the cave. Aura grabbed onto the wall for support. The sky ripped open, an ominous scar above her, red dripping from the wound, destroying trees and buildings below. The fracture in the sky was directly above the palace of Allegora. Aura could see it all from her high vantage point on the mountain, Verre and Baen joining her.

A black streak plummeted from the sky, hurtling toward the palace with frightening speed. It landed in a cloud of red, thick streaks of green spreading out and over the palace. Tiny specks fled in terror as the green consumed the palace.

Fear ate away at Aura, reducing Verre and Baen's voices to a dim echo in the back of her mind. Only one thought remained, screaming over and over in her head.

She was here.

Aura's worst fears had come true.

They had failed.

Blanca's sacrifice had been in vain, Aura betraying Cerise was in vain, saving the lives of their loved ones was in vain.

Everything had come to nothing.

If they wanted to fix this, it would mean war. A bloody, horrific war like none before.

One that might very well tear Atulau apart.

One that might finally make the lands unite.

It was time to face Rose's wrath.

Acknowledgements

Eekk! I did it! Still can't believe that I actually published a novel!

I'd just like to first of all thank my wonderful Beta readers (Isabel, Ashley, Mariana, Olivia, Anna—you guys rock!)

Secondly, my wonder editor, Abigayle! She helped so incredibly much in making this novel error-free!

Third, I'd like to thank my incredible proofreaders, Laine and Aria Nichols, for finding errors I would totally have missed! It's because of you two that I am confident this book is as polished as it can be!

I'd also like to thank my awesome family for putting up with my relentless coffee-drinking and computer-carrying. Without your patience and understanding, I wouldn't have been able to finish writing it.

I also want to thank all of my Wattpad friends and followers whose comments made me so incredibly happy. I'm so excited by how many of you enjoyed it! A special thanks to Joseph Ellis, one of my very first readers who has been nothing but supportive since!

Lastly, all credit goes to my Lord and Savior. He has given me the ability to write and has given me the zeal for it.

I'm not the greatest at remembering all the wonderful people who helped make this book a reality, so, to all those I might have missed, thank you too! And get ready for book two, Rose's Reign.

About the Author

Oceane McAllister is a fangirl-turned-author with a love of thunderstorms, black olives, and dancing shamelessly in the rain. A born-again Christian, her passion is to create clean, quality fiction for today's teens. She first started her writing endeavors at the age of eight and hasn't looked back since. Above all, she believes in writing original stories and refuses to ever write a love triangle into one of her novels. You can find her on Instagram, Goodreads, or at www.oceanemcallister.com.

STAY TUNED!

Rose's Reign, the grand conclusion to the Rose's War Duology, will be

available on Amazon soon!

Made in the USA
Middletown, DE
20 September 2020